The Bad Dad Club

Brandon Berry

1

Dedicated to:
Tracy – I hope you're happy
Mom and Ron – I know you're proud.

1

The cell phone on the bed above Gus began to vibrate, stirring him from sleep. Knowing what was coming, Gus groggily squirmed free of his covers and fumbled for his glasses. It was too late. Metal music blared from above him, filling the room and snapping him out of his groggy half-sleep. His roommate shifted in the bed above him but did not wake.

"Darn it, Art," Gus grumbled to himself. "How does that not wake you up?" He wriggled out of his bed, sat up, and reached up to the bed above him. After some feeling around, he found Art's phone, pulled it to his nose so he could see, and hit the "dismiss alarm" button on the screen.

Returning to his sanctuary, Gus grabbed his phone, lying on the floor next to his glasses. Hitting the power button, the phone came to life, blinding him momentarily. Gus squinted to read the time displayed in the middle of the screen:

"9:00 AM." He began his morning ritual of checking his social media: Facebook, Instagram, Twitter, and SnapChat. With nothing of interest happening, he grabbed his glasses as the vibrating above his head commenced again.

Gus crawled out of bed, stood up, and dismissed Art's second alarm. Stumbling over the excessive clutter in their room, he made his way to the closet. He grabbed his towel and soap and headed down the hall to the shower room. Because everyone was either asleep or still in class, Gus had the floor to himself, which he enjoyed. He could shower in peace.

Stepping into the water, Gus splashed his face to wake himself up. As the steam surrounded him, his mind began to wander. *What do I need to do today? Go to class. What day is it? Tuesday. So I have return papers to Written Composition at 12:30, then senior philosophy at 2:00 is cancelled. Thank God for study week! Just four more days until I graduate and get out of here. Four years has been long enough.*

Gus started mumbling to himself as he lathered up. "I should make sure Art gets up by noon. He probably has some late papers to make up for his psych classes. I may have to bribe him to keep him from playing PlayStation all day. I don't really have anything to do all day, so I can start reading *Lord of the Rings* again. I should also make a checklist to make sure I pack everything before I leave. First my books and miscellaneous decorations, then most of my clothes, and lastly my electronics and bedding. Oh shoot, Art and I also have to put our couch and bean bag chair into storage and rearrange our room. On top of sweeping and throwing away all of our trash. Oh well, we'll probably do that at the last minute as always. Knowing Neil, we'll get roped into helping him and Mikey move out too. It's a good thing Mikey and I aren't in any hurry to get home."

As he talked, Gus heard the door to the bathroom open. "Gussie, is that you? Are you talking to yourself again?"

"Shut up, Logan!" he shouted, shutting off the water. "You know, there have been several studies into the benefits of talking to yourself. I can show them to you some—"

"Nerd!" the voice yelled, cackling. The door opened and shut again.

Shaking his head and chuckling, Gus wrapped his towel around his waist, grabbed his soap and boxers, and left the shower. A full-length mirror hung in the hall next to the door to the showers, and he stopped in front of it. Water dripped from his dark, shaggy hair and down his tall, thin frame. Running his hand through his hair, he turned and continued down the hall to his room.

We Came as Romans blared from Art's phone again, but Art stirred enough to turn it off himself. Gus dried off and slipped into a pair of faded jeans and one of his many *Jurassic Park* shirts. He powered his laptop up and sat down at his desk to wait for Art to wake up.

It was nearly noon when the door opening behind him caught Gus's attention. He pulled his earphones out of his ears and turned to see Neil. His sandy blond hair was disheveled, as he had just woken up. He held a Nerf gun.

"Classic Art, sleeping forever," he said, raising the gun. He pulled the trigger, and a large red dart pelted Art in the chest. Gus and Neil laughed as Art stirred and started mumbling. Neil aimed and pulled the trigger again, hitting Art in the face. Suddenly awake, he grabbed the dart and threw it across the room.

"Get outta here!" he yelled, sitting upright. Neil shot him again, sending Art into a brief fit of rage. Throwing off his covers, Art jumped out of bed, grabbed a wooden katana from the couch, and chased Neil down the hall, shouting the whole way. Art returned to the room, grabbed his towel, and left for the shower room.

"This is what you get!" "I was just waking you up!" "Don't freaking come into my room and shoot me, you mook!" "Then wake up to your own alarm!"

The door across the hall opened, and Neil's roommate Mikey stumbled into Gus's room, shaking his head. He sat down at Art's desk and turned on his PlayStation.

"How shall we pester them today?" he asked mischievously, smirking. "I know. Let's find the most country song possible. Any suggestions?"

"It's not the most country, but it'll make Art rage like none other," Gus replied. "Kacey Musgraves, 'Follow Your Arrow.'"

"Diabolical!" Mikey opened YouTube, searched for the song, and soon Art's TV was blaring the song. Gus hid the controller in his dresser before following Mikey to his room and shutting the door behind them.

Mikey dug through his dresser and found baggy jeans and a Marvel t-shirt. He was in the process of spiking his black hair when the pair heard screaming from the hallway.

"What is this garbage?" Neil yelled.

"Is this who I think it is? Is it? If it is, I'm going

to kill someone! No, no! Aah!" Art started screaming to drown out the music.

"Turn it off, turn it off!"

"I'm trying, you mook! Shut up, Kacey Musgraves! I don't want to kiss lots of girls or boys! Don't tell me how to live my life!"

"Is there no God? Why did this happen? Who did this? What did we ever do to deserve such cruel and unusual punishment?"

"I bet I know who did it! And as soon as I find the controller and turn this garbage off, I'm gonna kill them! Oh thank God, that song's over!"

"But Art, another song is going to play automatically! And it's more Kacey Musgraves! Where the hell is that controller?"

"Wait! I can turn off the TV!" The music cut out suddenly, and Art and Neil shouted excitedly. "Now, where are those bastards?"

Art and Neil grabbed their weapons and burst into Mikey's room. He and Gus sat on the couch and nonchalantly scrolled through their phones. When their friends entered, they looked up obliviously.

"Yo, how were the showers?" Gus asked.

"You know what you did!" Neil shouted, firing his gun at the two. Mikey ducked, scooped up a pillow from the floor, and hurled it at his room-mate. He then reached under the couch, pulled out a Nerf gun, and deftly shot Neil in the forehead.

"I'm gonna kill you, you bastards!" Art charged forward and moved to stab Gus with the wooden katana.

"It's not my fault that my parents weren't married!" Gus replied, grabbing the sword and forcing it into the couch. He wrapped his legs around Art's waist as Mikey turned and shot him in the chest.

"Ow, fuck! My pump!" Art yelled angrily, pushing Gus's legs off him. "Good thing I needed a set change anyway. Fuck, that hurts!" Art disconnected the infusion set from his abdomen and left the room to attach a new one.

Gus and Mikey returned to their phones as their roommates dressed. Art wore black jeans, a gray band tee, and a blue zip hoodie. Neil donned skinny jeans and a striped V-neck. Neil and Gus slipped on their beanies while Mikey grabbed a windbreaker. After combing his unkempt black hair, Art joined them in the hallway, and the four of them departed for lunch.

In the dining hall, they grabbed their typical

meals of pizza, burgers, and fries and sat at a table. They stuffed their faces and talked loudly about YouTube videos, social media posts, new movies, and memories of school. As they talked, a short woman with blonde hair walked up to the table and sat down with them.

"Hey Kennedy," Mikey said.

"Hey Michael. How has your morning been?"

"Well," Art began, "I don't know about Gus, but I was rudely awakened by *somebody*." He glared at Neil. "That somebody broke into my room and shot me with a Nerf gun. So I had to chase this person down and shoot him back."

"Oh, and then a certain pair decided to torture us, so we had to get them back. Until one of them hit Art's diabetes, which was such a cheap move," Neil added. "I think we won by default."

"Says the one who got shot in the head!" Mikey retorted, high-fiving Gus.

"Boys!" Kennedy exclaimed. "You shouldn't roughhouse so much! Someone is going to get hurt! And hitting Art's insulin pump is a serious issue! Don't take it lightly!"

"Um, excuse you, we're men," Gus interjected. "We do manly things. Like sleep in, shoot people with Nerf guns, and eat unhealthy food."

"Yea!" Art agreed, high-fiving Gus. "Also it's

fine. The stupid tube gets caught on doorknobs and tables all the time. It hurts like none other, but it's fine. The pump is basically indestructible. And I needed a set change anyway."

"Besides, we're just waking each other up, playing video games, and watching stuff on Netflix and YouTube," Neil said. "We could be smoking weed in our dorms or sneaking women in to have sex, like some of the other guys."

"Guys," Gus said, shaking his head, "you realize that saying, 'People do worse than us,' is almost the worst excuse you can make, right? You can't justify what you do because it's more right than what somebody else does."

"Okay, Saint August," Mikey responded sarcastically. "We're talking about shooting each other with foam darts, not justifying the Holocaust." He laughed and lobbed a fry into Gus's drink. Gus quickly scooped it out and popped it into his mouth.

Kennedy rolled her eyes and signed. "You four are ridiculous. I don't know why I sit with you. August, Michael, are you two ready to graduate?"

"We don't have to talk about it!" Art and Neil yelled dramatically, jumping to their feet. They ran back into the food court. Kennedy shot them a disappointed look before returning to the conversation.

"Um, anyway, yea, I am ready," Mikey began. "CIU has been fun, and I've learned a lot, but it's about time I got out of here and moved to the next phase of my life. I'm not too excited about more responsibilities though. Bills and student loans are a pain!"

"Any idea what you'll do after graduation?" Kennedy asked.

"Nope, not a clue. Move down to Tennessee and marry Amber, I suppose. I'm not too worried about it. It'll pan out." Mikey shrugged.

"Michael!" Kennedy exclaimed. "You need to figure out what you're doing! You can't just go with the flow and put off important things like that!"

"Why not? We do it all the time," Art interjected, returning with Neil and several more plates of food.

"Honestly I don't know why I sit with you guys. You need to grow up. You can't procrastinate all your life. August, talk some sense into them. You're the responsible one!"

"Kennedy, they'll be fine. They'll grow up when they need to. Let them have their fun. Besides, they do a fairly good job of being responsible when they need to. If they didn't, they would've been failed out!"

"Yea, but if you fail to do your job and get fired, you can't just appeal to get it back," she retorted. "They need to learn responsibility."

"Bah, no we don't!" Neil said through a mouthful of cheese fries. "We know enough to get by. We know how to do the bare minimum. Why waste time and energy getting As in our classes when you can pass with a C or D and have more fun? You know what they say: Cs and Ds get degrees!" He glanced at Gus and laughed.

"Besides," Mikey added, "maybe we're more mature than you think. You don't see us all the time. You just see us at meals, when we're at our craziest! We may not be at Gus's level of mature over-achiever-dom, but we get stuff done."

"Is there really no chance of you doing something here?" Kennedy asked, turning to Gus. "Any way you could try to rub off on them before you leave?"

"I've done all the 'rubbing off' that I can," he replied. "If they learned anything, they won't let it show. They'll still be their crazy, irresponsible selves when people are looking. And if they didn't learn, they'll just have to learn the hard way. But don't underestimate them. Like Mikey said, they may be more mature than you think."

Kennedy rolled her eyes and sighed, exasperated. "Fine. I guess I'll see you boys at dinner." She stood up, gathered her dishes, and left.

"We're men!" Art yelled after her. "Whether you want to believe it or not, we are adults!" The group watched as she shook her head and left the cafeteria.

Gus continued eating as the others fell into conversation about *League of Legends*. Gus let his mind wander as he partially listened. He was deep in thought when Mikey nudged him.

"Dude, we're leaving."

"Oh yea, sweet. Back to the dorm?"

"Don't you have homework to take to Written Comp?" Mikey glanced the clock on the wall and saw that it was nearly 1:00.

"Oops. I'll just put the assignments in their mailboxes later today. I didn't even bring them with me." The four boys returned their dishes to the kitchen and headed back to the dorm. Even though it was a comfortable spring day, the wind blew constantly, making it feel brisk.

"What's up, Gus? You were in your head again," Mikey asked.

"It's nothing. I was just thinking about Kennedy's questions. We graduate soon, yet we have no idea what we're doing with our lives after college. I, the ostensibly responsible one, don't know what I'm doing. So I was thinking about what my options are."

"Dude, stop thinking so much!" Neil replied, slapping him on the shoulder. "And if you want to keep thinking, think about how we can have fun and enjoy these last few nights! And about when we're gonna go to the club and pick up chicks!"

"Shut up, Neil!" Gus punched him in the arm and laughed. "You and Art still have a year, and you'll probably wait until after graduation to think about any of this anyway."

"So what are your options?" Art asked, getting back on subject.

"Well there's always grad school," Gus began, and everyone groaned. "Yea, I'm not very interested in grad school, even though everyone wants me to go. I could just move back home and look for a place to live and work, too."

"True. I was thinking about the same thing. I need to find a place to live so I can get my teaching license, though. I have a meeting with Stew on Thursday, and we'll discuss that kind of stuff.

Maybe you should set up a meeting with Dr. J and do the same?" Mikey suggested. "You can bounce ideas off him, and he can offer some solid advice."

"That's true," Gus agreed. "After four years of class, I think he may know me well enough to help here!"

"I mean, what's the worst that could happen?" Art interrupted. "You have a meeting with one of the coolest professors on campus? I wish Dr. J was the head of my department. I'd meet with him every week to talk about everything!"

"I'll have to do that right now before I forget," Gus said, pulling out his phone.

By this time the boys were back in Art and Gus's room. Art powered up his PlayStation and started watching *Parks and Recreation* on Netflix, which he had been doing nonstop for the last couple of months. Conversation died as Art, Mikey, and Neil started playing *League*. Aside from the incessant mouse clicking and shouting in response to the game, Gus was undisturbed as he returned to his laptop.

2

Several hours later, Gus's phone vibrated. It was an email from Maybrook titled 'Last Minute Commencement Information.' Gus opened the email and skimmed its contents. It included times for rehearsal and reporting for commencement, as well as reminders about acceptable attire and behavior for the ceremony.

"Well what a surprise," Gus said sarcastically.

"What's a surprise?" Art asked, not looking away from his laptop.

"Maybrook sent us an email about graduation this weekend, and he finally revealed who will be giving the speech."

"Oh? Who?"

"Take a guess."

"You. Hawthorne. Mikey. Me. Donovan."

"Definitely not, thankfully no, absolutely not, never, and not after all of his shenanigans."

"Well then. He definitely wouldn't pick Cici.

That would be ridiculous," Art responded sarcastically.

"You're right, that would be crazy. It's some chick named Cecilia Domingo. Sounds pretty regal to me. I guess we'll find out on Saturday. Hopefully she gives a good speech."

"Oh yea," Art agreed. "What would you say if you were giving it?"

"Um, something along the lines of, 'Here's to never seeing you folks again. It's been real, but it hasn't been fun.'" As the boys laughed, a foam dart flew into the room and hit Art in the head.

"Again? What the hell?" he yelled. Keeping his right hand on the mouse, he opened one of his desk drawers and pulled out a Nerf gun.

"I got this, bro." Gus took the gun, jumped out of his chair, and darted toward the hallway. "Why did you shoot my roommate? I'm gonna kill you!"

"Whoa man!" Neil exclaimed. "I was just trying to mess with Art's game!"

"Well now you have to mess with me!"

Gus fired a dart as Neil sidestepped out of the doorway and backed toward the bathrooms. As Gus exited his room, he ducked to avoid another dart from Neil. He cocked his gun and charged down the hallway, shooting a couple of darts at

Neil as he ran. Neil stepped into the doorway of a vacant room and raised his gun to retaliate, but Gus reached him, grabbed his wrist, and pointed the gun at the ceiling.

"What are you gonna do now? Huh?" Gus shouted cockily. "I win this round!" He stuck the barrel of his gun into Neil's stomach and pulled the trigger. Neil's eyes widened as he dramatically fell to the floor to feign death.

"Et tu, Brute?" he muttered. "Then fall Caesar." He collapsed and went limp.

"Art! I killed him for you!" Gus yelled, turning to head back to his dorm.

"Good! He deserved it!"

As Gus walked down the hall, he felt a dart strike him in the back. He dropped to his knees and turned to see Neil go limp again. Gus let the gun fall from his hand and collapsed in the middle of the hallway. He and Neil remained motionless for several minutes.

"Hey guys, when's dinner? I'm starving!" Mikey yelled from his room. "Also where are our roommates?"

"Um dinner is right now! And last I knew, Gus killed Neil for shooting me." Art stood up and slipped on his shoes. He and Mikey stepped into the hallway and noticed their roommates down the hall.

"Gus, no!" they yelled dramatically, running down the hall. Art started to shake his roommate and help him to stand as Mikey poked Neil with his foot.

"Way to go, stupid, you killed our favorite roommate," Mikey grumbled. "Now get your butt up so we can go eat."

"Fine, fine, I'm up!" Neil took the Nerf guns back to his room and returned with his and Gus's shoes. "Any idea what's for dinner?" Neil asked as the two slipped on their shoes and followed Mikey out of the building.

"Does it matter? We'll probably just get the same thing as usual." Mikey laughed and slapped Neil on the back, and everyone laughed. They hurried to the cafeteria, as the wind made the evening air quite chilly without jackets.

Inside the cafeteria, Neil and Art jumped immediately in line for pizza, burgers, and fries, while Gus and Mikey weighed their options first. Seeing country fried steak, they immediately grabbed plates covered in mashed potatoes, steak, and gravy. They went into the dining hall and claimed a table.

Art and Neil joined them quickly, with plates of their normal meals in tow. The four of them chowed down as people continued to enter the room. They were soon joined by a group of guys from another wing of the dorm, led by a bearded young man named Donovan.

"Hey boys!" he said, trading fist bumps with the group. "So Gus, Mikey, excited for graduation? Only four more days!"

"You know it, Donovan!" Mikey exclaimed. "Any idea what you'll do afterward?"

"Go back home and look for a job! Any plans for you guys?" Mikey and Gus shook their heads. "No matter. Have some laughs here before we leave!"

"Speaking of laughs, are you pulling any last-minute pranks before you leave?" Art asked. "You should go out with a bang!"

"I have something big planned for the ceremony. But until then, I'm just winging it. In fact, I think I just got an idea." Donovan glanced at Art, smirked, and started whispering to his friends. They started grinning mischievously.

"Care to let us in the loop?" Neil asked excitedly.

"Just go with the flow, boys. This will be good," Donovan replied, returning to his food.

Dinner progressed without incident. The table laughed, joked, and reminisced on the various pranks they pulled. Everyone kept getting up to get more food, but as time went on, Gus noticed that Donovan and his friends hardly ate any of their more recent plates.

"Donovan, are you doing what I think you're doing?" he asked, glancing at Donovan's plate for emphasis. The mischievous smirk returned to his face as he turned to his friends.

"I think it's time for some fun, don't you boys?" Donovan gave a thumbs-up to his friends, and they all stood up.

"Food fight!" Adrian, the tall, skinny boy next to Donovan, yelled, grabbing a handful of potatoes from his plate and throwing it across room. It splattered across a group of freshmen girls, who screamed before a couple of them stood up and scooped food in their hands to retaliate.

Mikey and Neil jumped to their feet immediately and flipped the table onto its side. Donovan and his friends did the same with the adjacent tables, creating a barrier. The boys all ducked behind it as handfuls of potatoes, salad, and stir fry flew across the room. Other groups around the dining hall were following suit, setting up tables as barriers and tossing food.

"Donovan! You realize how much trouble we'll get in for this, right?" Gus had to yell to be heard over the roar of guys grunting and girls screaming. Donovan either did not hear or ignored him, focusing on lobbing half a country fried steak at a round table of junior girls. It knocked over a cup of juice, which splashed all over the table and the girls.

"Lighten up, dude!" Adrian replied. "What are they gonna do, withhold our diplomas? We worked hard and paid a ton of money for those!"

Before long, the president of the school marched in, a few of the cafeteria workers at his heels. The students scrapped piles of food off clothes, tables, and the walls and floors to throw again. Donovan and his friends had discovered dozens of condiment bottles on a table in the corner. After tossing them around the room, everyone was running around squirting ketchup, mustard, and barbecue sauce all over each other. Initially hesitant, even Gus had gotten involved.

"Enough!" President Maybrook's face was bright red. After he shouted, everyone in the room immediately stopped and stared at the ground. They looked around the room and began to assess the situation.

"Whose idea was this?" Maybrook demanded, looking intently at every individual. The whole room seemed to hold its breath. "Is any-body going to take responsibility for this?" The room remained silent.

"It was my idea." Donovan raised his hand and looked Maybrook in the eye. His friends walked over to him and mumbled their compli-ance. Maybrook approached them quietly.

"Boys. I know you've pulled a lot of pranks during your time here. I appreciate how you have enjoyed your time here and how you've made others' time enjoyable. However, this is crossing the line." The president spoke sternly, shifting his gaze between Donovan and his friends. They all stared at the ground, motionless and wordless.

"Because you're graduating this weekend, there isn't much that I can do. So, as punishment, you boys will clean the cafeteria all week, after every meal. I will get all of your names before you leave tonight, and I will personally check to make sure you are cleaning when mealtimes end."

"Yes sir," Donovan and his friends re-sponded.

"Additionally, you boys will not walk at grad-uation this weekend. You will receive your diplo-mas in the mail in the near future. Do you under-stand?" Maybrook approached the group and pulled a small notebook and pen out of his suit-coat.

"Understood, sir." Maybrook began taking their names and home addresses. He then divided the group into three pairs and appointed them cleaning responsibilities. As Maybrook left the room to open the janitor's closet, Donovan glanced at Gus and smirked.

Gus smacked Neil in the arm, as he was standing closest to him. "Let's give them a hand. Start picking up dishes."

Neil nodded and yelled at Art and Mikey to do the same. Donovan and his friends righted the tables and started mopping the floor. A handful of them, carrying buckets of soapy water and rags, got to work scrubbing the tabletops and walls. Meanwhile, the rest of the students in the dining hall filed out, snickering amongst themselves.

"I ask that you boys leave. These guys will take care of their mess." Maybrook had returned to the room to supervise the cleaning, and he stared at Gus.

"Yea, get out of here. Go clean yourselves up," Donovan sneered. "Thanks for the help though!" He smirked again.

"We'll just finish picking up the dishes, then

we'll leave," Mikey explained. Maybrook nodded and started barking orders at Donovan and his friends.

Before long, Gus, Art, Mikey, and Neil walked out of the cafeteria into the chilly night air. Between dinner, the food fight, and clean up, they had killed about two hours in the cafeteria. Now they were covered in food and condiments from head to toe.

"All of the showers are probably taken," Gus said. "The freshmen are probably cleaning themselves off after the fight."

"Classic freshmen," Neil laughed. "We probably shouldn't just walk through the lobby dripping gravy and ketchup all over the place."

"Good call. We'll go in the back." Mikey gestured to the right, and the group cut across the grass to go around the building.

Reaching the back door, the boys stripped down to their boxers and left everything in a pile outside the door. They darted inside, grabbed their towels and soap, and raced to the showers.

"Would you look at that?" Neil exclaimed as they stepped inside.

"I guess the freshmen showered while we were cleaning up the dining hall," Art suggested. The room was steamy, with water and food all over the floor, but none of the showers were running. The boys quickly stripped and jumped in.

"So who's washing our laundry?" Mikey shouted above the sound of rushing water.

"Better question: *how* are we washing our laundry?" Art retorted.

"Well I think Art's out. He never does his own laundry anyway; his parents wash it every week," Neil responded.

"Challenge: last person in the shower washes the laundry!" Gus yelled, laughing.

"Deal!" The four boys began quickly scrubbing their bodies and washing their hair, trying to remove all the food residue. As much of it had begun to dry, it took several cycles of lather, rinse, repeat to get it out.

"Ow! Soap in my eyes, soap in my eyes!" Neil began to scream dramatically. The boys heard thudding from his shower as Neil punched the wall. All four of them busted out laughing.

"Done!" Mikey yelled. Gus was right behind him, shutting off the water and wrapping his towel around his waist. Stepping out of his shower, he saw Mikey, also in his towel, leaning against the wall.

"Come on, ladies! It's either Art or Neil now!"

Gus taunted. As he finished the sentence, the water in Art's shower shut off.

"Nope, not me! Have fun washing our laundry, Neil!" the boy exclaimed, laughing.

"You should probably rinse the clothes off in one of the showers first," Mikey suggested. "But chances are high that all of that stuff is probably ruined." Neil and Art stepped out of their showers, and the four of them returned to their rooms and got dressed.

As Neil started the laundry, Art turned on his PlayStation to play *Call of Duty*. Mikey sat down on Art's couch and grabbed a controller to play. Gus turned his computer chair to face the TV and picked up another controller. Neil joined them shortly afterward for a few rounds of zombies.

Around midnight, Neil came into the room with his arms full of clothes. He threw them on the couch next to Mikey, who began digging through the pile and sorting the clothing. Gus saw that everything was stained with splotches of gray, red, and yellow, so he stuffed his clothes into the back of his dresser.

A guy from down the hall, Quentin, walked into the room and saw what they were doing. He disappeared and returned with a bowl of popcorn to watch the spectacle.

After another hour, Gus handed his controller to Quentin and crawled into bed. Pulling *Fellowship of the Ring* out from under his pillow, Gus curled up under the covers and read until he drifted off to sleep.

3

"Mikey! Gus! Come here!" a voice shouted from down the hall. Gus recognized it as Lee, one of their resident assistants. Setting his laptop on Mikey's couch, he followed Mikey down the hallway. "We're in Logan's room!"

Several doors down, they entered the room. Inside, they found four men. Lee and his twin brother Jordan were there. Both were tall and skinny, standing eye-to-eye with Gus. Jordan let his thick, black hair frizz into a sort of afro, while Lee kept his cut short. The other two guys were Logan and Arin. Logan was portly and had long, curly blond hair, while Arin was tiny by comparison, with short red hair.

"Take a seat, dudes," Logan said, gesturing toward the couch. They sat down as Jordan closed the door and sat down between them.

"As one of your RAs, I am obligated to tell you that you cannot leave," he said, rustling their hair.

"So either fail one of your classes or start a new degree."

"Actually don't do that," Arin interrupted. "Or else you'll end up like me and Logan."

"Yea," Logan agreed. "We've been here for five years, changed our majors a handful of times, and failed a dozen or so classes. Don't do that."

"Yea Jordan," Lee said, throwing a small football at his brother. Jordan caught the ball and tossed it back.

"You guys know what I mean!" he argued. "The floor is going to be so different without these guys. It's going to be weird. And who's going to keep Neil and Art in line?"

"Yea we know," Gus said. "Quentin keeps bringing it up. And Marcus keeps asking how my last full week on campus is going."

Mikey chuckled and shook his head. "Oh those guys. We've barely known them eight months and yet they act like we've known them since birth. I'm gonna miss them, though."

"Well that's more or less why we called you in here," Jordan replied. "We've met with Tyson, Charlie, and Luke already, so you two are the only seniors left."

"Well, aside from us," Arin mumbled, nodding toward Logan. "But we're super-seniors, and we aren't graduating until next year. You guys are all leaving for good next week. So we wanted to have a little chat."

"So let's get down to business," Jordan said. "We're gonna skip the cliché questions about how college was and if you're ready to graduate. I'm sure you've gotten more than enough of those already."

"So instead, let me ask you two just one question," Lee added. "What have you learned about yourself during your time here at CIU?"

"Yea Gus, what have you learned about yourself?" Mikey repeated, turning toward him dramatically.

"Fine, whatever, I'll go first. I discovered that I have overvalued my education for most of my life. Not that education is bad or studying is wrong, but I let it consume my life. It wasn't until I met Art and Neil that I figured that out. After I moved over here with Mikey, I started skipping classes to run to Bloomington and staying up late to finish an anime. I failed assignments and settled for Bs on my transcript. And I think that has made a huge difference in my life."

"I mean, you sure as hell had a lot more fun!" Logan remarked. "I can't tell you how many times Jordan and I have come back from a late-night IHOP run and heard the four of you mani-acs laughing hysterically in one of your rooms."

"And I've heard plenty of rumors of your an-tics," Arin said. "Like sneaking into the admin building and switching people's offices."

"Or taking a game of Assassins so seriously that you get banned from the library and the caf-eteria. And kicked out of the coffee shop and the ladies' dorms," Jordan added.

"What about that time they painted windows across campus for Christmas?" Logan chuckled to himself. "Though I hear that was Donovan's idea, but props to you guys for taking part in it. It made campus more festive."

"Anyway," Lee interrupted, "I'm glad to hear that, Gussie. Hopefully you can keep that balance between work and play when you don't live with the guys!"

"I mean, it was my idea to help Donovan paint the school," Gus mumbled. "And I always orga-nized Assassins."

"Shut up, my turn!" Mikey announced, shov-ing a pillow into Gus's face. Gus retaliated by re-peatedly hitting him with the pillow while he spoke. "I learned that my head is full of knowledge and information because that's most of what the educational system teaches. But what

I don't have is wisdom or practical application for the stuff that is in my head. Especially with theoretical stuff in teaching, I knew *what* to do but not *how* to do it or how it would actually *work*." Mikey paused to tear the pillow from Gus's hands and throw it across the room.

"So what have you done to work on that?" Arin asked.

"Student teaching really helped this last year," Mikey answered. "And I've gotten involved at a church and a daycare to practice teaching methods on various age groups. And it taught me a valuable lesson: there is no substitute for experience. I can read the most recent books and structure my lessons according to their input, but that lesson would fail because I forgot to consider the most important part: the audience.

"I have to know the people I'm teaching: age, maturity, ways of thinking, and everything else that I can learn. It's the same for any profession, not just teaching. You don't help people by treating them like numbers and statistics. You help people by treating them like human beings. They have their own thoughts, emotions, dreams, goals, scars. Once you start to consider all of that, you can begin to teach, counsel, lead, or do whatever you want. That's when you'll succeed."

"Whoa, that got deep," Jordan sighed. "I was hoping you'd just say that you found a partier buried under all that academic nonsense or something."

"Well, with such amazing RAs as us," Lee chimed in, "how could you expect anything less from these young men?"

"True that!" Arin agreed, giving Lee a high five. "Anyway, that's enough of the serious talk. I just have one question: when's the wedding, Mikey? I'm disappointed that we haven't gotten our invitations yet!"

"It's August 6th," Mikey answered. "Also I sent out 'save the dates' and invitations like two months ago. Have you checked your mail?" The four guys exchanged sheepish looks before shrugging and laughing. "But anyway, there's still a lot to do between now and then. Wedding planning, moving away from home totally, finding a house and a job, and everything else. But at least school will be done for both of us!"

"Well take away the wedding, and it's pretty much the same for me," Gus agreed. "I also have grad school to consider. Everyone wants me to go, and I have a couple of ideas. But I'll talk to Dr. J sometime tomorrow or Friday. But there's so much to do, and nobody gave us any form of handbook on being an adult!"

"So true," Lee agreed. "I'm not at all jealous of that. It is kind of cool that you guys get to move on to something bigger and better, but the whole 'being responsible' thing just doesn't sound appealing to me at the moment."

"Good thing we have another year or two until we have to deal with that!" Arin added. "You two will have to stay in touch and give us some advice!"

"We'll see what we can do," Gus replied. "You know, I think the hardest adjustment won't be paying bills or working full time or any of that. School has basically been a full-time job for sixteen years now, and I know how to budget money. Those may take some getting used to, but I think living alone will be the weirdest."

"Oh yea," Mikey agreed. "We've had three crazy years on this floor, surrounded by you guys nonstop. It'll be weird to have my own place without the constant yelling, body odor, and presence of thirty dudes. Actually, now that I think about it, I can't wait to get out of here!" The guys all laughed, after which the room fell silent.

"Jeez, I can't believe it's already graduation time," Gus mumbled.

"Seriously," Lee said. "It feels like we all just

moved up here a couple months ago."

"It's crazy how fast time flies by nowadays," Mikey agreed. "I swear that I just graduated high school like last week. But here I am, getting ready to graduate college."

"I remember when you both first visited our floor three years ago," Logan said.

"Yea! Art invited you two over to our floor movie night. You guys were so quiet and aloof, especially Gussie here. Now you're just as crazy and loud as the rest of us." Arin chuckled and shook his head. "It's almost like you aren't even the same two guys anymore."

"It's dinner time!" Art yelled from down the hall. He and Neil started shouting back and forth, alternating between gibberish, threats to stab each other, and announcing dinner.

"Well, that's our cue." Gus stood up. The rest of the guys joined him and started taking turns hugging him and Mikey.

"Thanks for coming to the floor," Logan said.

"Definitely. It was cool watching you two grow up and embrace our craziness," Arin agreed. "Don't lose that craziness."

"Have fun being an adult! But don't forget to be a kid sometimes," Lee added.

"And if you need anything, don't hesitate to

ask," Jordan said. "We love you guys, and we have your back if you need it."

"Thanks!" Mikey and Gus replied, opening the door and joining Art and Neil.

4

After dinner, the group took a trip into town to Wal-Mart. Once inside the store, Neil and Art made a beeline for the electronics, while Gus and Mikey grabbed a cart and headed to the grocery section. Going aisle by aisle, they snagged various snacks off the shelves and tossed them into the cart. They darted around the store, setting off to find Neil and Art a few minutes later with a variety of junk food.

"What did you guys get?" Neil asked without looking at them. He and Art were gazing intently into the display cases full of video games.

"Plenty of chips, candy, cookies, and pop," Mikey responded. "So how are we splitting all of this? Who's buying what?"

"Eh, we'll figure it out." Art shrugged, and Gus rolled his eyes.

"Art can buy the Mountain Dew. I grabbed four cases of the stuff," Gus answered.

"Dibs on the chips!" Neil yelled, still not looking their way. He walked around the display racks to look at the available movies, Art at his heels.

"Fine. Gus can get the cookies, and I'll cover the candy," Mikey continued. "Anything look interesting?" He weaved his way through the display racks along with Neil and Art. Gus pushed the cart slowly after them.

"Nah, just the same old stuff," Art mumbled. "It's almost like we were just here a few days ago. We just needed extra stuff to celebrate the end of the year!"

Neil led the group away from the electronics towards the toys. They ignored all of the aisles until they found the Nerf guns. Though they had collectively purchased every gun available, they always visited this area. Sometimes they looked, others they were compelled to expand their collection or needed replacement darts.

"En garde!" Gus turned in time to see Mikey toss three foam swords into the air, brandishing a fourth in his hand. Catching them, Art and Neil wordlessly made one team while Gus shuffled over to Mikey.

"We'll leave the cart here. Ten minutes. Head or torso shots are instant death," Neil explained.

"If someone slashes your arm or leg, you lose that limb."

"We'll start in one minute," Gus added, pulling out his phone. "Return here ten minutes after that. The pair with the most limbs left wins."

"Bathrooms are off limits," Art interrupted. "No hiding out. Just sneaking around."

"Start in sixty. Go!" Gus turned on his heels and power-walked away from the group. Mikey followed him for a few aisles before darting off on his own corner of the store to start.

Gus took his place in the sporting goods section. When time was up, he immediately moved toward the middle of the store. He tiptoed toward the clothing racks, scanning his surroundings. He barely stepped into the walkway surrounding the clothes when he glanced left and saw Neil standing there, grinning ear to ear.

"You always come here, Gussie," he taunted, approaching slowly. Gus raised his sword and glanced around quickly. There was no telling where Art was.

Neil swung first, and Gus parried. They continued swinging and blocking, taking turns being on the offensive and defensive. Meanwhile, they moved throughout the area, down the nearby aisles and around the clothing racks.

Backing out of an aisle, Gus saw sudden movement to his right. Reacting quickly, he deflected Art's sword away from his face. But it provided enough distraction for Neil to jab forward and scrape Gus's left arm. Holding it behind his back, Gus backpedaled to put some space between him and the pair.

"Way to miss, stupid!" Art grumbled.

"Dude, his arms are like eight feet long. They're way easier to hit," Neil countered, shrugging. The two turned to Gus and advanced quickly.

"Too bad you couldn't get one of my legs, or even my right arm!" Gus teased. "I can still take the both of you easily until Mikey gets here."

With a grin, Art and Neil bounded forward, swinging wildly. Gus sidestepped into the nearest aisle, reducing the amount of space around him. Art and Neil continued their assault, swinging and jabbing their swords vigorously. Gus swung wildly to deflect their strikes.

With all of his attention focused on his friends, Gus did not realize that he was running out of space in his current aisle. The space around him suddenly opened up, and Art and Neil smirked confidently. Deflecting an attack from Art, Gus backpedaled quickly to distance himself. He glanced around for Mikey, wondering what was taking him so long. Deciding to surprise his opponents, he tightened his grip and charged.

Art was the first to react, stepping forward and raising his sword. Unfortunately, he was neither tall nor quick enough, as Gus jabbed his sword into Art's chest. Art dramatically fell to his knees and dropped his sword as Neil lunged at Gus. Once again, the two traded blows. Art had returned to his feet and followed them, quickly shouting commentary over the fight.

"Gus deflects a downward strike by Neil! Then he counters with a jab aimed at Neil's neck! Neil dodges and swings upward, but Gus parries it and tries another jab!" As this all happened, Gus was slowly backing up, leading Neil along the clothing section.

Suddenly a foam sword appeared from within the nearest clothes rack, slashing upwards across Neil's back. Neil was unable to hide his surprise as he turned to see Mikey emerging from amongst the Carhartt jackets, grinning from ear to ear. Chuckling, Neil dropped his sword and fell to his hands and knees in defeat.

"And Mikey defeats Neil with a surprise attack! Mikey and Gus win!" Art cheered, helping Neil to his feet.

"Good game," he panted, shaking hands with Mikey. "Nice job taking us both, Gus."

"You gave me a run for my money," Gus responded, catching his breath. "Dude, how long were you waiting there?"

"Oh you know, just the whole time," Mikey said, laughing. "I watched you and Neil duke it out and followed you the whole time. I saw Art's sneak attack and the whole 2-v-1 situation. It was pretty intense!"

"Jerk!" Gus punched him in the arm. "You could've jumped in and given me a hand sooner! We could've dominated 2-v-2! Next time I'll just take all three of you on myself!"

"Manchester!" Neil shouted. "We'll wipe the floor with you!"

"Don't be like that, Gussie! You were doing so well without me!" Mikey responded. "I was getting ready to jump in when the two of you started moving my way. Then I just decided to finish it with a surprise attack."

"Fair enough, but I'm not backing out on that Manchester. We should get our stuff and head back to the dorm." Gus started walking back to the Nerf aisle to grab their cart. "Anybody break or damage their sword?" They all inspected their foam weapons and found no sign of use as they reached their cart.

Returning the swords to their shelf, the boys sorted through their snacks. The put each person's purchase in different corners of the cart to make check-out easier. Then they made their way to the nearest register and loaded the conveyor belt. They recognized their cashier as Jenna, a tall strawberry blonde woman who often worked during the evenings and nights when they ventured to Wal-Mart.

"Well if it isn't my favorite boys!" she greeted cheerfully. "*Ça va*[1]?"

"Hey Jenna!" Mikey responded. "We're doing well. I don't remember how to say that in French, or else I'd say it."

"*Bien* would suffice," Gus said. "Is your French still doing well?"

"*Oui*," she replied. "I spend at least half an hour on Duolingo daily, so I'm still fairly fluent. Plus, I've started teaching myself German too."

"That's crazy!" Neil said. "You need to stop being so smart!"

Jenna shrugged. "I can't really help it. I needed a hobby, and I didn't want anything boring. So I chose to learn languages! You guys do

---

[1] "How are you?"

anything crazy tonight?" She winked at them. Most of the evening and night employees knew that they tended to have fun while shopping, but it only bothered a few of them.

"Nothing too crazy, just some sword fighting!" Neil answered, pantomiming such a fight. "We grabbed some Nerf swords and had a quick 2-v-2 match. Gus and Mikey won."

"Sounds like fun! I don't see any swords here, so I assume you didn't break anything?"

"Nope, nothing broken!" Art answered.

"You know we'd clean it up if we did!" Neil added. "We always pick up after ourselves. And we buy anything we break."

"Seriously, we have like two dozen broken Nerf swords in the trunk." Mikey laughed.

"That's a valid point," Jenna replied. "When does school let out?" Mikey swiped his debit card to pay for his groceries, and she continued swiping their items.

"Well Gus and I graduate on Saturday." Mikey turned and high-fived him. "These other two bozos have finals next week, but they'll be done by Thursday."

"Wow, you boys have grown up so much! Who will come in here and liven up the place once you leave?" Jenna stuck out her bottom lip to feign pouting.

"You'll still have us for another year!" Art assured her. "We'll have to befriend some of the freshmen and let them in on our shenanigans!"

"As if! You'll never replace our charm and sense of humor!" Gus puffed out his chest. "This place will just fall into monotonous despair."

"*C'est dommage²!* I guess I'll just have to find a new, more exciting job! So, Gus and Mikey, do you have any plans for life after college?"

"Wait, I'm supposed to have a plan?" Gus asked, staring blankly. "I guess my plan is to come up with a plan. I'll let you know when I figure it out!"

"Wow, who would've thought that Gus would be the unprepared one?" Mikey mused. "I actually have something of a plan. Amber is in Tennessee, and she graduates next weekend. I can move down there until we get married."

"Nice! You guys will have to come back and see little ole me once you make it big! What are you two going to do with them gone?" She turned to look at Neil and Art as she handed Neil his change and continued checking them out.

"Cry," Neil answered immediately. "For at

---

² "Too bad" or "That's a shame."

least a week."

"And by 'week,' he means 'year,'" Art added. "I'm not really sure. We haven't thought about it too much. We still have the summer, so it won't really be weird until school starts in the fall. We'll figure it out."

"I'm sure we'll Discord from time to time. Play video games and chat on Facebook all the time. We got this. We may have to grow up a bit though, since they're the mature ones," Neil mumbled, grimacing.

"*C'est la vie*[3]," Jenna said. "If it's any consolation, I'll be here at your friendly neighborhood Wal-Mart if you want to hang out! And, I'll be returning to CIU in the fall!"

"Manchester!" Neil interrupted. "Come back, Jenna!"

"Oh Neil, you wouldn't slap me even if I didn't," she replied. "Besides, that depends on the school accepting me back. But if they do, I'll gladly be there!"

"That's great!" Mikey exclaimed. "We've missed you there, even though you were only around for a year."

"Oh yea!" Art agreed. "When you come back,

---

[3] "Such is life."

we'll definitely hang out all the time!"

"*Ça marche*[4]!" she said. "I look forward to it! But in the meantime, you guys should do something fun this summer, before you all split up. Something big, crazy, and fun that you'll remember for years."

"What do you have in mind?" Mikey asked.

"You could book a cruise or make a trip to Universal Studios," she suggested. "Go backpacking in Europe. Visit Japan, since I know you guys are crazy about all of that anime stuff. Rent a cabin in the mountains in Tennessee for a week. Something you guys wouldn't normally do in a summer!"

"All good ideas," Gus remarked, swiping his debit card. "Except maybe the international ones. I don't think Neil has a passport. But the others could be fun!"

"Jeez, did you guys get enough snacks?" Jenna asked, ringing up their Mountain Dew. "Are you going to eat all of this in just a week?"

"Of course!" Art replied, handing her some cash. "We eat all the time. And if we don't eat it all, we'll just divide it between us for the summer."

---

[4] "That works!"

Jenna chuckled and handed Art his change. "Let me give you guys a quick hug before you get out of here!" She walked around the register and hugged each of them in turn.

"See you around, Jenna!" they yelled, waving as they walked away.

"See you guys!" she yelled back. "Gus, Mikey, best of luck after graduation! Neil, Art, I'll see you guys next semester! Have a great summer!"

They loaded their groceries into the back of Mikey's SUV and piled into the vehicle, with Gus riding shotgun. They sped out of the parking lot and headed back to campus.

"It's crazy how close we are to graduating," Gus said, turning to Mikey.

"Seriously!" Mikey agreed, turning down the radio. "Pretty soon we'll be paying bills, working our 9-to-5 jobs, and living boring adult lives!" Everyone started to wretch and gag.

"Thank goodness I'm not graduating this year!" Neil interjected. "I'll gladly take another year of being a kid! What about you, Art?" Art shouted his affirmation, and they high-fived.

"You mean you'll take another year of being irresponsible, right?" Gus teased. "You know, playing *League* all the time, never doing your homework until the day that it's due, and sleeping through classes."

"Oh come on, we don't do all of those —" Neil began. He paused when Gus shot him a skeptical look. "Yea, you're right. But we have so much fun! Unlike you, who just reads and does homework all the time." Gus turned around and punched him in the chest.

"And you forgot to mention all of our Nerf wars," Art added. "We'll totally make the best adults someday. 'Someday' just isn't 'today.'"

"You're right," Mikey agreed. "It's probably in two or three years, when you two finally manage to graduate!"

"But just think of the shenanigans we can get into with the freshmen next year!" Art replied. "Especially once Jenna gets here!"

By this point, Mikey turned into the campus parking lot and found a parking space. The boys grabbed their groceries and headed to their dorm rooms, still talking about all of the antics they had pulled. Back in their rooms, they divided the snacks and drinks evenly between the two rooms and put everything away. Gus was taking off his jeans and shirt to read and relax before bed when Mikey walked in with a six-pack of root beer.

"All right, boys, I think tonight calls for a

toast," he explained, tossing bottles to Gus and Art. "I bought twelve bottles of this stuff, so we can do three toasts before graduation. I'm sure we'll go out sometime before then, so we can grab more for a post-ceremony toast."

"Yea, cheers and what-not." Neil walked into the room and belched loudly. He dropped an empty bottle into the trash and grabbed another from Mikey. He and Art twisted the tops off and chugged their drinks without another word.

"That went about as well as we should've expected," Gus admitted. Mikey shrugged, and the two downed their root beer as Neil left the room. He returned with another bottle, already half empty.

"Well, I guess I have to kill Neil," Mikey said nonchalantly. He dropped his bottle in the trash, turned, and chased Neil down the hallway.

5

"Hey Doc!" Mikey said, stepping into Dr. James Stewart's office. Bookshelves lined the walls of the room, overflowing with books. Manila folders bursting with papers covered half of the professor's desk, with a corner dedicated to several pictures of his family.

"Mikey!" Stew exclaimed, jumping out of his chair and hurrying around his desk. He pulled Mikey into a tight hug. "Take a seat. I bet you'll sit on the futon."

"You know me!" Mikey replied, sitting down. Stew sat on the arm of one of his office's armchairs to talk. "When's the last time you jumped on this thing?"

"Well it's been a little while. Don't tell anyone, but I'm getting old!" he said, laughing. "I think I jumped on it about a month ago. Grading you and your classmates' senior research projects stressed me out, so I took a break."

"Understandable! I nearly went insane writing that thing! But I couldn't jump on the futon. I'd be worried about scraping my head on the ceiling."

"Well I'm a little too short for that, and I don't have much left up here to lose," Stew replied, rubbing his balding head and laughing. "So what can I do for you?"

"Well, to put it simply, you can teach me how to adult since I graduate in three days!"

"I can do my best. What specifically can I do? Have you figured out where you're going to live yet? I know that was an issue when we last met a few weeks ago."

"I have a fairly good idea," Mikey began. "Amber has a job lined up in Tennessee, so I plan on moving down there this summer and looking for a job."

"Where in Tennessee? I can look into schools and put in a good word for you!" Without warning, Stew stood up and jumped over the empty side of his desk. He began typing furiously at his computer.

"Nashville. She has family down there, so I can live with them if I can't find a place to live right away. But I would like to be able to secure a job as soon as possible, then I can start looking for houses for us."

"That reminds me!" Stew exclaimed, glancing up from his laptop as he typed. "When is the wedding? And am I invited?"

"I put your invitation in your mailbox last week, Doc," he replied, chuckling. "The ceremony is August 6th. I know you'll be there, so I wasn't too worried about you sending in your RSVP. I'll have spots saved for your whole family.

"Oops, I guess I should check that more often. Are you even saving spots for my sons-in-law and grandchildren?"

"Of course. I have ten spots reserved for the Stewart family."

"You're awesome! Okay, here's what I've found. Three elementary schools looking for special education teachers. I know two of the principals fairly well, so I will shoot them emails with your contact information. They should get in touch with you sometime in the next couple of weeks."

"Sweet, thanks so much! One other thing: what are your thoughts on grad school?"

"If you need or want it, go for it. If you don't think you'll need it, put it off until you need it. But as a teacher, you should hold off on getting a Master's anyway. You'll find it harder to get a job because schools have to pay you more if you have one. Also, make sure the Master's degree suits your needs better than an alternative. You may be able to get another Bachelor's and do exactly what you want, which would be easier.

"But most importantly, don't bury yourself in student loans. Too many students fly through undergraduate and graduate school, borrowing tens of thousands of dollars. Then they spend the rest of their lives struggling to make loan payments each month. Life is a marathon, so don't shoot yourself in the foot before you even start running."

"That's pretty much what I was thinking," Mikey said. "But if I decide to get another degree, what would you recommend? What do you think best suits me?"

"Hmm." Stew stopped typing and stood up, pacing around the room as he thought. "I would say psychology, perhaps with some extra study in abnormal psych. That would help you understand how your children's brains operate more clearly, and it opens up the possibility of being a professional counseling in the future."

"Psychology-slash-abnormal psychology, got it," he mumbled, typing into his phone. "That's everything I wanted to talk about, so I'll let you get back to work." Mikey stood up and walked to the doorway before pausing and turning around.

"Hold up," Stewart interrupted as Mikey put his phone in his jacket pocket. "I have a question to ask you. What was the best part of your time here at CIU?"

Mikey paused and stared out the window as he thought of an answer. Finally, he chuckled and responded. "The people I met. Most of them were drastically different from me, in background, life goals, and personal beliefs and opinions. Butting heads with a couple of them drove me nuts and often made life here miserable. But meeting students and profs who think so differently from me made me reconsider my own beliefs and look at things from another perspective.

"But most of all, it was the people like me who made it worthwhile. If not for them, I would've left after freshman year. They listened to and understood what I thought and felt. They validated those things too; not once did they accuse me of being dramatic or pitying myself. They responded to my distress and pain as if it was truly real to me, even though I always thought they had it worse than me."

"You're talking about August, aren't you? Him, Art, and Neil?"

"Yea. Gus especially, but they've all helped in their own ways."

"I'm quite familiar with Gus," Stew mused. "I've taught him in a couple of classes. He's so quiet, but whenever he speaks or writes, he does so with an air of deep understanding and wisdom. That young man has a gift, perhaps one of the greatest gifts that a human being could ever possess. And it seems that he's been able to share that gift with you."

"What gift is that?"

The professor sat back in his chair, crossed his arms, and stared at the ceiling. "How do I put it into words? He understands pain. Not just that he's had some hard times and knows what it's like to suffer. That is certainly true, but that's only part of the gift. He understands the nature of pain. He knows deeply that pain is real and strong. Pain isn't on a scale; something is either painful or not. So there isn't any 'lesser' or 'greater' suffering. People don't have it 'better' or 'worse.' Everybody has it badly, everyone feels pain. You simply have to understand how and why. And when the pain comes, when it demands to be felt, you must let it. That's his gift. If the two of you could teach others to think and act that way, you could change more lives than with any career path."

Stewart paused and chuckled. "But that's just the musings of this old man. Now get outta here, Mikey. You have a lot to do in the next few days! I look forward to seeing you graduate. If I don't talk to you then, I'll see you in August. Oh, and pass my congratulations on to Gus when you see him!" The professor walked over to the door and opened it. Mikey followed and paused in the doorway.

Stew grinned as he stood in front of Mikey and placed his hands on the young man's shoulders. "I remember the day that I first met you. Three years ago, when you came to my office to talk about switching your major from business to teaching. You were so passionate about helping special education students, and that passion has only grown. You've performed well in all of my classes. Not just regarding grades, but you've demonstrated mastery over the material. You've grown and learned a lot since we first met. I'm blessed and honored to have helped you grow into the young man you are today. Always remember: I'm proud of you."

Gus climbed the stairs to the second floor, where Dr. Jameson's office was. As he opened the door from the stairwell, he saw the professor standing at the vending machine in the corner of the hallway. The machine whirred, and a bottle of Dr. Pepper popped out.

"Oh hey Gus!" Jameson said as he turned around. "I was just grabbing a drink before our meeting. Do you want something?" Before Gus could respond, Jameson thrust the first bottle into his hands and turned back to the machine to get one for himself.

"Thanks Dr. J. How much have you had to-day?" he asked, twisting the bottle open.

"Um, this is my first bottle," he replied, taking a drink. "But I had a large fountain drink from the gas station already."

"You might have a drinking problem," Gus joked as they walked down the hallway.

"Nah, I could stop if I was allowed to. Doctor's orders, y'know?" Jameson glanced at Gus and winked.

Jameson stepped aside and gestured for Gus to enter the office. The desk sat inside the door, giving the professor a good view into the hallway to see everyone who walked past. A number of Post-it notes covered his desk, reminding him of appointments and tasks. His reading chair sat in one corner, a large lounge chair with a standing lamp behind it.

"Black or white?" Jameson asked.

"Black, as usual." They walked to the other corner and sat down on opposite sides of the small table there. A chessboard sat on the table between them, ready to be played. Jameson made his first move as they started talking.

"How many times have students beat you?"

"How many do you think have beaten me?" Jameson replied.

Gus sighed and shook his head. "You had to redirect that question? You couldn't answer that one? Um, I'd say at least one student a semester."

"Hmm, close. In my twenty years here, I have played countless games, with students of various skill levels. I've had to teach quite a fair amount to play so we can have our meetings. But then many don't take the game too seriously. They make moves but never really try to win. That's the roundabout way of me saying that I have lost fifty-three games in my time here. So an average of more than one game a semester."

"Has anybody beat you this semester?"

"Not yet. I have a couple more meetings this week, so maybe someone will. Honestly, I'm surprised you haven't beaten me yet!"

"Maybe I'll manage to do that today," Gus

said, smirking confidently. "Anyway, I wanted to talk about the possibility of graduate school."

"What are your thoughts on the subject?" Jameson asked.

"Well there doesn't seem to be much to do with a Bachelor's degree in philosophy. It seems to be a springboard into future studies in philosophy, law, or something. So going to grad school is almost a requirement if I want to do something other than teach or flip burgers."

"Well there's nothing wrong with flipping burgers. Or teaching for that matter! You'd make a great teacher. But I digress. What do you want to do with the rest of your life?"

Gus shook his head. "You know, there's a fundamental problem with that question. It suggests that one must choose a career that he will hold from the end of college until the day he dies. But that's not the way life often works. No matter where you go or what you do, there are opportunities for upward mobility. Plus, you can get more education or receive an unexpected job offer and change your career path at any point in life. So when you ask what I want to do with my life, you should really ask what direction I want to proceed with my life, not what destination I want to reach."

"You truly excel when it comes to semantic arguments," Jameson responded, laughing heartily. "What would be the ideal direction for your life, then?"

"I want to help people. I don't know how, but I want to make people's lives better. That's all that really matters to me."

"Hmm." Jameson paused to take a drink of Dr. Pepper. "What is one thing in this world that you would change if you could?"

"Divorce," Gus answered immediately. "My parents' divorce has had a larger impact on my life than anything else. And I know plenty of people my age and older who are emotionally ruined because of it."

"I figured you'd say that," Jameson said, grinning. "What can you do about that?"

"I can stop it. I'm not really sure how, but maybe I can find a way. I guess becoming a marriage counselor could help. But then there are couple who would seek an attorney before even considering counseling. So maybe I could become a divorce attorney. Or," Gus continued, clapping his hands excitedly and grinning, "I can become a pro chess player. Checkmate."

"By golly, you're right! I hardly even realized what you were doing. That was a good game!

Why haven't you beaten me all semester if you could do it so easily?"

"I was waiting for our last game," he admitted. "I knew we would play either this week or next, if only for one last game before I left. So I spent the last few years learning how you play and memorizing a number of quick wins."

"I think you'd make a great lawyer with such a sharp mind," Jameson said. "You notice details and always think a few steps ahead of others. Really, you'll be great at anything you do, with such a quick and eager mind. So that begs the question: is being an attorney something that you can see yourself doing?" The two began resetting the chess board.

"I don't know," Gus muttered after a moment. "I hadn't thought of that option until just now, so I haven't had time to weigh pros and cons."

"Well take a moment to think about it now. We both know it won't take you long. Think about what you'd do as an attorney and compare that with what you want to do."

"Well from what I understand, one of my primary tasks will be helping couples to divorce. Settle issues of belongings, child custody, alimony, and child support. So I would basically tear families apart legally, causing the exact pain that I want to treat and prevent. Maybe I don't really want to be an attorney after all."

"Okay, so begin with the end in mind," Jameson replied. "Your ultimate goal is to treat and prevent that pain. How can you do that?"

"The idea of studying counseling is still appealing. I may need to take some psychology classes before I proceed with that, but I can manage that. But I think one of the best ways to reach that goal is to reach those who have already experienced divorce. Kids like me. If I can teach them to take their pain seriously, I can guide them to face the wounds they've received and begin the healing process. And if they can understand their own pain, I can provide them with advice and resources to make better decisions in life. I need a career path that allows me to do all of that."

"What if I told you that there's a field that lets you do all of that? Counseling families and individuals, meeting kids from various family types, providing them with resources to succeed in life. This field can also allow you to intervene in dangerous or negative situations, such as abuse and neglect, and put the children in safer environments. Does that sound like something you would be interested in studying?" The professor finished his drink and tossed the bottle into a nearby trashcan as Gus processed the information.

"It certainly sounds appealing," Gus began, "but I want to do more research before I make a decision. I need to look into options for pursuing such a degree and possibilities for career paths if I decide to go that route. This isn't a decision to make lightly!" Gus laughed and stood up from the table.

"That is true," Jameson agreed, standing as well. "But it's also a decision that you don't need to rush. Don't worry about the future too much. If it comes, you'll take care of it. If it doesn't, then no amount of planning or worrying will make a difference." The pair reached the doorway to Jameson's office and paused.

"Oh, I have something to give you before you leave." Jameson retrieved a blank envelope from his desk as Gus stepped into the hall.

"What's this?"

"It's the secret of life," he replied. "When you read it, you'll understand. But it's the one thing that has made everything worthwhile. If you remember this secret, you can succeed at anything in life. You can read it anytime: as soon as you leave, ten years down the road, or anywhere in between."

"Noted. I'll keep it safe," Gus said, taking the envelope. "Also, are you going to tell me what that mystery profession is?"

"Nope." Jameson chuckled as he began slowly closing his door. "That's for you to figure out yourself. Now get out of here!"

The door clicked shut as Gus headed downstairs, wondering what the envelope contained. Before he stepped outside, he decided to find out. He carefully tore the top of the envelope open and pulled out a single strip of paper with four words written on it.

"Live actively, not vicariously."

6

When Friday morning came, Gus and Art slept in, having turned off their alarms. It was around 11 when whispering and muffled movement stirred Gus from his sleep. Pulling back the curtain around his bed, he squinted to see what was happening, half-asleep and without his glasses.

"Attack!" Gus hardly had time to register that Mikey stood over him before he swung a round object toward him. Without his glasses, Gus could not see what was happening, but he felt it almost immediately.

"What the eff?" he shouted as ice cubes struck his bare torso. "What in the world is wrong with you people? I'm going to murder you!" He continued screaming and flailing in bed, pushing the ice to the floor and crawling out.

As he did this, Art began to flail violently above him, shouting profanities and similar promises to murder Neil. Standing up, Gus saw Neil at the foot of Art's bed with a bucket. He had pulled back the covers and dumped ice on Art to wake him up. Turning his attention to Mikey, Gus glared for a moment and gave chase as Mikey darted out of the room.

The back door out of the dorm was closer, so Mikey ran for that. Not caring that he was only in boxers, Gus followed. Once outside, Mikey took off across the lawn. He barely made it fifty yards before Gus caught up and tackled him to the ground.

"So you wanna wrestle?" Mikey taunted, squirming on the ground. "Just like old times!"

"Nope, I wanna strangle you," Gus responded, chuckling. The boys rolled around in the grass, each trying to pin the other down.

They rolled a few times before one of them ended up on top. Then the bottom person would squirm loose and start rolling. Whenever one got to his feet, they crouched low to the ground and walked slowly in a circle before someone lunged and started the wrestling again.

Neil came out of the dorm as Gus got behind Mikey and jumped onto his back, wrapping his legs around his waist. The pair fell backwards to the ground as Art darted out of the dorm with a baseball bat. Neil stopped to laugh at Gus and Mikey, giving Art a chance to start smacking him defiantly with the bat.

"Get a room, guys!" Neil taunted as they continued rolling. "Also, we should get ready for lunch. Then we can play *League*."

"Sounds like a plan," Gus gasped, sprawling out in the grass.

"Ha!" Mikey panted. "That's a forfeit! I win again!"

"It's more of a, uh, tactical retreat," Gus retorted. "I'll win next time."

"Manchester!" Mikey shouted, standing and helping Gus to his feet.

The boys returned to the dorm, dressed, and headed to the cafeteria to eat. After getting their meals, they sat down at an empty table. Soon, they were joined by Kennedy.

"Hey boys!" she greeted. "How's your study day going?"

"Well we slept until eleven. Then we were rudely awakened by some bozos throwing buckets of ice into our beds." Art glared at Neil as he answered.

"Boys! Why would you do that?"

"It gets better," Mikey interrupted, smirking.

"Oh yes," Art agreed. "I chased Neil around

the floor and beat him with my bat. He tried to hide in his room, but I carded the door. Then I started beating him again."

"Meanwhile, I chased Mikey out of the building in my boxers. We wrestled in the lawn for a few minutes. It was a good time."

"First, why would you throw ice at your friends?" Kennedy turned to Neil and Mikey.

"More importantly, where in the world did you get buckets of ice?" Gus asked.

"Funny story about that," Neil answered. "We may or may not have broken into the maintenance shed on the edge of campus to get the buckets. Then we sneaked into the kitchen to fill them with ice. We carded your door and woke you up."

"As for Kennedy's question," Mikey added, "why not? We thought it was funny, and it did not disappoint!"

Kennedy sighed and turned to Art and Gus. "Why did you attack your friends?"

"Um, because they started it!" Art again glared at Neil. "And they totally deserved it."

"Boys, what am I gonna do with you?" Kennedy shook her head dejectedly.

"Let us graduate and leave CIU?" Mikey suggested.

"Oh boys. You need to grow up," she said.

"You can't keep playing pranks and goofing off for the rest of your lives."

"I think we can," Neil replied. "We can stay young at heart. Have fun with our wives and kids. Play games with our co-workers, maybe prank them occasionally. There's no need to be all uptight and mature all the time."

"You, mature? That's a good one!!" Gus teased, laughing heartily.

"I'm afraid to ask, but I have to," Kennedy began. "Have you been studying and finishing up your assignments?"

"What's studying?" Neil asked, stuffing cheesy fries into his mouth.

"I saw a post on the Internet one time about it being a combination of 'student' and 'dying,'" Art replied. "I'm already constantly in a state of almost dying because of my pancreas. I don't need any more of that!"

"Then you have Mikey and me," Gus added. "We're finished with all of our undergrad stuff, so we can relax, play video games, watch Netflix. It's pretty great."

"You should keep Art and Neil in line then! You have plenty of time and ability to do so!"

"Both of those are true," Mikey mused. "But

they're both adults. If they want to fail more clas- ses, they're going to do it. We can't force them to do anything. They'll grow up one of these days, when they need to. Wait until next semester; I'm sure you'll be surprised by how mature they be- come when we leave!"

Shaking her head, Kennedy finished her last few bites of food and stood up. "I'll see you boys later. Gus, Mikey, get ready for graduation. Art and Neil, study!"

"Okay, Mom," Art teased. The group finished eating and left the cafeteria.

"What are we going to do today?" Mikey asked. "Play *League*? Watch *Parks and Rec*? Cards Against Humanity? Nap?"

"You know what we haven't done in a while? Gone spelunking," Gus answered. "We could do that until dinner."

"Yes!" Art cheered. "I love *Spelunky*!"

"I'm going to torment *all* of you so much," Neil said.

"Is there any other way to play?" Mikey joked, taking off running to the dorm.

7

Several hours later, Quentin had replaced Mikey and Gus in playing *Spelunky*. Mikey and Gus had gone to the auditorium to rehearse the commencement ceremony. They were gone for several hours, returning in time to head to dinner.

"Oh hey guys," Quentin said when they stepped into Neil and Mikey's room. "How was rehearsal?"

"Shut your face and focus, Q!" Art yelled. "You're going to kill us all!"

"Isn't that the point of the game?" he retorted, setting down his controller. "Oh snap, it's dinner time! Let's roll!" He darted out of the room and headed to the cafeteria.

"You know, I'm not really feeling the caf tonight," Gus said as Neil turned off the PlayStation. "Let's ditch campus and go get some good food."

"Perfect!" Mikey agreed. "Where do we want

to eat?"

"Well, Steak n Shake is the best place in town," Art answered. "It's cheap, delicious, and fairly quick. Plus they have milkshakes, and they're open all night."

With no other suggestions, they hurried to Mikey's SUV and sped across town to the restaurant. Their waitress, a young blonde named Claire, seated them at a booth in the far corner of the room.

"Here we are, away from most of the crowd in case you guys get rowdy again," she said, passing out menus. "How are you boys doing tonight?"

"We're good!" Gus replied. "How are you?"

"Bored!" she groaned, rolling her eyes. "It's so dull in here today."

"Well worry no more!" Mikey asserted. "We're here, so you know it'll get a little crazy!" He gave her a wink and chuckled.

"What can I get you guys to drink?" Claire pulled out her pad and pen and looked at Gus.

Mikey and Gus ordered Dr. Pepper, while Art and Neil got Pepsi. Claire walked away to get their drinks as the group opened their menus.

"I don't know about you guys," Neil started, "but I'm super hungry. I might get like two or three meals!"

"Same girl same," Gus agreed. He looked over the various burgers in front of him.

"So let's chow down then!" Mikey was grinning ear to ear. "We'll make this our 'Last Supper' and eat until we're stuffed!"

Claire returned with their drinks and took their orders. The group ordered several burgers and chicken sandwiches, a couple dozen shooters, and cheese fries.

"I'd say you boys are hungry!" Claire teased, picking up the menus.

"Yea, you could say that! Graduation is on Saturday, so this is our last supper together," Art explained.

"Well this is the first I've heard of that," Gus mumbled quickly, causing the group to laugh. "But I guess it works."

"Aww, you boys are leaving me?" Claire replied, pouting. "Well congrats on finishing college! I'm still uncertain about what I want to do, so I'll probably just work until I figure it out."

"No rush!" Neil assured. "There's no point wasting your time and money if you don't know what you want to do. Plus, you only graduated last year! So many kids our age rush into a college major and end up changing half a dozen times because they don't know what they really want to study."

"So true! I'll get these orders in and come back to chat a bit," Claire said, smiling as she turned and walked toward the kitchen.

"One other thing!" Neil yelled quickly. "Grab a glass of water and come back!"

"Okay?" Confused, she walked away and came back as requested.

"I want to start our night with a toast since I botched the one earlier," he explained. The five of them raised their glasses. "To the best friends we could ever need. Through everything, these people have been there to laugh and cry with us, and even to make fun of us when we do something stupid. May these friendships never fade, no matter how much distance separates us or how much time passes."

"To friends!" they agreed, clinking their glasses together. Liquid splashed onto the table as they each drank deeply.

"You guys are great," Claire said. "Now I'll actually go put these orders in, unless you want to do anything else?" She winked at Neil.

"No, that's it. I just wanted to include you in the toast, since you're a friend!" he replied. She grinned and walked away.

"So what are we doing tonight? It's our last

night as undergraduate students," Gus asked. "We need to close this chapter of our life perfectly. So we need to make these last twenty-four hours count."

"We can lock ourselves in our dorms and play video games all night," Neil suggested. "Pig out on the snacks we bought, pull an all-nighter, watch our favorite YouTube videos."

"That could be fun," Mikey responded. "Except two of us have a long, boring graduation ceremony to attend in the morning. And Maybrook wouldn't be happy if we slept through it, even if we did show up."

"So no all-nighter. Fine, why not just do everything else?"

"What are you guys talking about?" Claire pulled a chair to the end of the table and sat backwards on it, crossing her arms on the back of the chair. She leaned in to join the conversation.

"We were discussing our plans for tonight," Gus explained. "So far the plan is to lock ourselves in our rooms and play video games."

"That could be fun. But here's a bigger question: what are your plans for after graduation?" Claire locked eyes with both Gus and Mikey. "My manager has a thing that she likes to do for graduating seniors."

"How often do you get seniors in here?" Neil interrupted sarcastically.

"You'd be surprised," she answered. "We see a lot of kids your age in December. And we serve a ton of high school and college grads in May."

"Makes sense. There's not much else to do here in town," Gus said. "So what is this thing that your manager does?"

"I'll be right back." Claire spun out of her seat and walked off without a word.

The group jumped back into brainstorming plans for their last night: taking an impromptu road trip, pranking Donovan and his floor, starting a campus-wide Nerf war. Neil suggested pulling the fire alarm in the middle of the night and breaking into the president's office to replace his office photos, while Art clung to Neil's original idea. Mikey discussed the possibilities of camping and streaking across campus.

As the ideas got more ridiculous, Claire returned with a giant tray full of food. She set it all on the table, letting the guys sort it out themselves, and quickly brought drink refills. As the group started eating, she sat down, stole a few fries from Neil, and pulled some paper from her apron. She unfolded it and passed a half-sheet to each of the boys, saving one for herself.

Looking at his paper, Gus saw that it was blank. No lines or instructions. Confused, he looked at the others' reactions. Their papers seemed to be blank as well, so they turned to Claire, who was handing out pens.

"Here are the instructions," she began. "Paint a picture of your future. You can write lists or complete sentences. You could even doodle some pictures. However you do it, think about life five, ten, fifteen years down the road and ask yourself, 'Where do I want to be? What do I want to do? Who do I want to become?' Then, on the bottom or the back or another sheet of paper, you can start writing steps for getting there."

"Give us an example," Neil requested. "Also, why do Art and I have to do this? We don't graduate until next year."

"You boys are in college," she said. "You should think about your future before senior year. I'm sure Mikey and Gus can attest to this: few will ask you what you want to do when you're a freshman or sophomore. A few might ask you as a junior, but everybody you meet will want to know what your plans are once you become a senior."

"It's true," Gus confirmed.

"Seriously. No one said a thing, but as soon as

we started last fall, everybody was interested," Mikey added. "Not only did they ask, but they also told us what we 'should' do."

Claire unfolded her sheet of paper, flattening it on the table. "This is my plan. My manager asks new employees to make five-year goals, and she encourages us to update them regularly. So I wrote things like 'find my passion,' 'start attending college,' 'write 100 new poems,' and 'go on a road trip with friends.' You can put goals for your career, education, relationships, or leisure. It's your future, so make it what you want. Think of it as a bucket list."

With a smile, Claire winked and grabbed one of Neil's shooters, stuffing it into her mouth as she walked away. Neil threw his hands in the air and shouted gibberish. He threatened not to tip her, but she just chuckled and disappeared into the kitchen. Shaking his head, he turned back to the food and his friends.

"You should've expected that," Mikey taunted.

"Classic Claire," Art agreed, "always stealing our food. Or, more specifically, always stealing *your* food."

"So are we actually doing this thing?" Neil asked, mouth full of fries. "Because I have no idea what I'm doing this weekend, let alone five years from now!"

"It could be interesting," Gus began. "But I think we should do it when we're ready. You know, think about our futures, talk it out with friends, mentors, and family, and then try to make some plans."

Nodding in agreement, conversation waned as the boys devoured the food before them. As the food disappeared, they slowed down their eating. Gus looked at each of his friends in turn. Each seemed to be deep in thought, and Neil and Art kept glancing at Mikey and him. Finishing his last handful of fries, he took a swig of Dr. Pepper and cleared his throat.

"So what's up, guys?" he asked. The table remained silent as the others finished their food and started stacking their plates.

"All right, I'll spill," Neil mumbled. "I hate awkward silences. It's weird to think that you guys will be gone next year."

"I was thinking the same thing," Art seconded. "We've been here for years, so it'll be weird without you. And then I got to thinking about Claire's pieces of paper and what I want to do with my life after I graduate."

"It is weird to think about." Mikey stared at

the sweat dripping down his glass. "But we'll stay in touch. Life after college isn't just work; there will be plenty of chances to hang out and have fun like old times!" He looked up and grinned.

"That's fairly true," Gus agreed. "We'll have to work around our schedules and take time off work, but we can do it. We'll find new rhythms of life so that we can still talk and play games together regularly."

"And I guess we'll have to grow up next year, since you guys won't be here to be the responsible ones," Art added. "Just a bit though. Like doing homework the day before it's due instead of a couple hours beforehand."

"Looks like the food was good!" The guys looked up to see Claire with four milkshakes on a tray. "I think I know you guys well enough to surprise you with your favorite shakes for your 'Last Supper.' On the house, too!"

"Oh sweet! What did you get us?" Neil asked, grinning smugly.

"Peanut butter cup for Mikey, M&Ms for Gus, chocolate fudge for Neil, and cookies and cream for Art," she replied, passing out the shakes. She handed out spoons and straws and piled the plates on her tray. "How did I do?"

"Perfect!" Mikey exclaimed. "Thanks!"

"No problem," she said, smiling. "I'll bring you guys your checks."

Claire walked back to the kitchen as the boys began devouring their shakes. Gus and Mikey paced themselves, taking small bites. Art and Neil shoveled spoonfuls of the dessert into their mouths quickly.

"Ahh, brain freeze!" Neil yelled. He clutched his head with one hand and pounded the table with the other, shouting continuously. The others started laughing so hard that they could not talk or breathe.

"For one thing," Gus wheezed, "slow down!" He paused to catch his breath. "Secondly, stick your thumb on the roof of your mouth!"

With his thumb in his mouth, Neil's yelling became more muffled. It did not take long for him to stop grimacing and wipe his thumb off on his jeans. Art and Mikey finally stopped laughing and caught their breath. Claire returned with their checks as they finished their milkshakes.

"Need anything else, boys?" she asked. "How about some aspirin for your brain freeze?" She patted Neil on the head and chuckled.

"You saw that?" He turned bright red and covered his face.

"I think the whole restaurant saw," she replied. "But it's okay. I'm sure you've done much more embarrassing stuff. Anyway, you have your checks, so you're free to go anytime. Mikey and Gus just have to promise me one thing."

"Of course, anything," Mikey said. Gus nodded in agreement.

"Don't forget about your friends when you graduate and move on to whatever is next in life," she told them, locking eyes with Gus and then Mikey. "Pinky promise!" She stuck her hand out toward the two of them.

"We promise," they answered, interlocking their pinkies with hers.

"Wait, does that include Neil?" Gus asked. Neil punched him in the arm as the group laughed and stood up.

"Good. Have a good life! Come back and visit sometime!" Claire gave each of them a tight hug and walked away.

8

Around midnight, Gus stripped to his boxers and crawled into bed, intending to fall asleep early. His stomach began to twist into knots as he lay in bed, staring at Art's mattress above him. Art and Neil's voices grew louder as they returned with Mikey from hanging out with Quentin and Marcus.

"You still awake down there?" Mikey asked as they entered his room. Gus heard him sit down on his couch and assumed that Neil had taken a seat at his desk.

"You know it. I can't stop thinking about tomorrow." Gus mused, remaining in his bed.

"Aww," Neil teased, "do you want me to come cuddle with you and make you feel better?" He stood up, made his way to Gus's bed, and pulled back the comforter that hid him.

"Only if you want to die tonight!" Gus retorted. He picked up the Nerf gun beside his bed and shot at Neil's face. "This is my sanctuary! Nobody enters without my permission!"

"Fine, fine!" Neil said, returning to his seat.

"Nobody messes with Gussie's happy place," Mikey teased. "Anyway, I can't believe it's been four years already. I'm not ready to move out, get a job, and pay bills. I'm not ready to adult!"

"No thank you, that just sounds gross!" Neil interrupted. "I think I'll hold off on that."

"How different does it feel from high school graduation?" Art asked without looking at them. He typed quickly on his laptop.

"Completely different," Mikey replied. "At least after high school, we knew there was college, so we didn't have to grow up yet. There were still summers to spend with friends and responsibilities we could shirk without major consequence. Now all of that is gone. Last year was our last summer vacation."

"Plus the whole idea of graduation feels different," Gus added. "Back then, your closest friends were more superficial. You knew them because you were trapped together for 40 hours or more a week. Now our friends are people who have stuck with us through everything. Parting ways with you guys will be so freaking difficult. Thinking about it makes me want to cry and give up on graduation."

"Yikes," Art muttered. "That's no fun. I'm not quite that emotional yet. I think it will all hit me sometime next month or even as late as August. You know, when it really sinks in that you two aren't coming back."

"What do your families think about you graduating?" Neil asked. "Also, speaking of, are they going to be here?"

"Mine will," Mikey said, sighing. "The whole family is coming down in the morning."

"Why didn't they come down today and get a hotel room or two?" Neil replied.

"Too many kids. If they can avoid staying in hotel rooms, they will. Even with Jenny and Suzie to help babysit, having just four of them in a single room is chaotic. Dad will wake them all up really early so that they sleep in the car. It's so much more peaceful that way, trust me!"

"You still didn't answer the first question," Gus teased.

"What do they think of me graduating?" Mikey repeated. "Who knows? I don't talk to them much when I'm not home, so I guess I'll find out. I imagine Mom is bummed that I'm fully moving out, but Dad is probably eager for me to take over all my bills."

"Classic parents," Art added. "Those are very typical reactions. What about you, Gus?"

"Well, that's part of how it's different from high school," he began. "I had grandparents attend that ceremony. But now Mom's parents are both dead, and I haven't spoken to Brock's mom since then. But Mom and Dave got into town while we were at Steak n Shake, so they'll be at the ceremony."

"Nice!" Neil said. "What do they think? Are they excited?"

"I think so. Maybe a little nervous because I don't know what I'm doing this summer or next fall, but I'd say they're proud of me for finishing." Gus paused suddenly. "Now if only Brock was proud. That would be nice."

Silence filled the room. After a moment, Mikey reached under the comforter and patted Gus's mattress gently. "We feel you, bro. We all wish that our dads were proud of us."

"And that they'd tell us so," Art mumbled.

"And that they were able to tell us," Neil mumbled sullenly.

"Yea," Gus said. "That's the thing about people like us. What should be our greatest moments become our lowest, all because of one person. All of our victories feel empty because our fathers don't recognize them."

"So true," Art agreed. "But we still win. Even if they don't see it, we still win."

"And we can continue to win," Neil continued. "You've already shown that! You finished high school at the top of your class, and now you're doing the same in college! That's a win if I ever saw one."

"Exactly!" Mikey threw Art's comforter onto his bed, exposing Gus. He then reached over and rustled Gus's hair affectionately. "So keep your head up. Not because everything is good, but because you're doing all right."

"Thanks guys," Gus said, smiling. He crawled out of his bed enough to grab the blanket from Art's bed. As he did, a bottle under Art's chair caught his eye. He paused, then quickly pulled himself onto the couch next to Mikey. "I have an idea for our last night on campus, but we need lots of root beer. And I need pants."

9

Gus's alarm startled him out of sleep at 7:00 the next morning. Groaning, he silenced the alarm and felt around for his glasses. Above him, Art snored loudly.

Gus crawled out of bed and headed to the showers. As he stepped into the hallway, Mikey opened his door. Nodding groggily at each other, they proceeded to the shower room and stepped into the streams of hot water.

"Graduation is stupid," Mikey yelled over the sound of rushing water. "Who decided this whole ceremony thing was a good idea?"

"Seriously," Gus agreed. "We rehearsed this stupid thing for three hours yesterday. Why do we need to be there this early?"

"I guess this gives people time to take plenty of pictures," Mikey suggested. "You know, in their fancy gowns with all of their friends and professors. And Maybrook will probably want to run through the ceremony one last time."

"Yea, too bad I'm not interested in any pictures. Except maybe with Jameson. And with you guys and my parents, obviously."

"I think I'll pass on the family photo," Mikey replied. "We should wake Art and Neil up before we leave. They'll want to be at graduation."

"True. They'll want to see Donovan's prank and our little stunt. How did that go, by the way? Is everything in place?"

"Oh yes," Gus answered, grinning. "Neil and I were out until about 3, but we took care of everything. It's gonna be great."

"Good. Any ideas what Donovan has planned for today?"

"Hopefully it's nothing like his banana hammock shenanigans at our dorm meetings. That would be quite crude. But I trust that they'll do something memorable." Gus shut off the water and wrapped his towel around his waist.

"I guess we should go get dressed," Mikey mumbled, stepping out of the shower.

"Let's just get this over with. I'm so ready to be done."

"We're gonna need a hardcore nap after graduation." Mikey laughed and followed Gus down the hall. They entered their rooms, shook their roommates awake, and went to their closets to find clothes.

Gus grabbed khakis and a white dress shirt. Tucking in his shirt, he slipped a navy vest over his shirt and tied a matching bowtie around his neck. He found his navy Vans and put those on his feet. Meanwhile, Mikey dressed himself in black slacks, a blue dress shirt, and a blue and black stripped tie. He was tying his dress shoes when Art and Neil returned from their showers. As they dried off and dressed, Mikey and Gus got ready to leave.

"You sure you're up for this?" Neil shouted.

"Absolutely," Gus answered. "I've been running it through my head constantly. I even dreamt of it last night. They'll never see it coming. Not from me."

"You better be! That took too much time to set-up for you to flake on us! When does graduation start, again?"

"Nine o'clock, stupid," Art replied. "We should be there around 8:30. Take a selfie together, then we'll need to find our seats."

"Good plan," Mikey said. "Meanwhile, we have to leave. Like, now." He and Gus stepped out into the hall with their black gowns on. Tucking their caps under their arms, they headed down the hall, out of the building, and across campus to the auditorium.

Inside the building, they found their classmates crowded in the lobby, already wearing their gowns. As they looked around, President Maybrook approached them.

"Boys," he greeted. Gus turned and found himself face-to-face with the president's scowl.

"Good morning, President Maybrook," they replied.

"August Millburn and Michael Kilroy," he mumbled, checking their names off on a clipboard. "Congratulations on finishing your degrees. A couple more hours, and you both will be home free."

"Thank you, sir," Gus replied. "We look forward to being done."

"As you should. You all worked hard to get here. Just a few formalities and then you'll never hear from me again. Except for alumni association business. Which reminds me." Maybrook turned abruptly and walked to the auditorium doors. "Seniors! File inside and take your seats! I will give you last-minute instructions momentarily." The room immediately fell silent, and everyone entered the auditorium and sat down in the first few rows of seats.

"Ladies and gentlemen," Maybrook continued. He stood a few feet in front of the group. "Congratulations on making it to graduation. I know you all have worked hard to get here, and I am just as eager to get this over with as you are. If you all do as we rehearsed, this ceremony will proceed smoothly and finish within two hours. I will open the ceremony with a greeting, after which I will call Ms. Domingo to the stage to deliver her speech. After that, I will return to the podium to pass out diplomas. After a final word from yours truly, you will be done. I will then dismiss you all to the lobby, where your friends and families will soon join you. Understand?"

"Yes sir!" the group said in unison.

"Do we need to run through the ceremony again?"

"No sir!"

"Good. It is now about 8:20. Meet backstage in twenty minutes, at 8:40. Dismissed!" Maybrook walked away quickly, leaving the seniors to mingle with each other.

Heading to the lobby, Gus and Mikey found Art and Neil waiting for them. Art wore a purple dress shirt with black jeans and gray Vans. He refused to tuck his shirts into his pants because it bothered his insulin pump. Neil wore designer jeans, a simple white dress shirt, loosened black tie, and black dress shoes. He also had donned his black beanie.

"Look who made it! And actually dressed up!" Mikey taunted, jabbing Neil in the arm.

"Shut your face," he responded. "How's Maybrook this morning?"

"Just typical Maybrook," Gus said, laughing. "We have to head backstage in twenty."

"Is the root beer still in place?" Art asked in a hushed voice, eyes darting around the room.

"Yea, it's there," Gus affirmed. "I can't wait to see the look on Maybrook's face when we pull this little stunt."

"Oh yea," Neil agreed. "But I think it'll be quite tame compared to whatever Donovan has planned! He tends to go all-out with his pranks."

"This is gonna be one graduation ceremony to remember!" Art pulled out his phone. "How about a couple of selfies to commemorate?"

"Here, use my phone instead," Gus offered, reaching under his gown into his pants pocket. They quickly took a series of selfies, both serious and goofy.

"You better send those to us," Art said. "And don't you dare post any of them! Those are for us, not everyone else." Gus laughed and agreed.

"Well we should go take our seats," Neil interrupted. "You guys have fun. And don't forget to do your thing, Gus!" Without another word, he and Art walked into the auditorium. Gus and Mikey left the lobby and headed backstage to wait for the ceremony to begin. Maybrook entered the room shortly afterward.

"Okay seniors!" he bellowed when the clock read 8:40. "Line up in order, just like yesterday. The dean of students will begin the ceremony with the Pledge of Allegiance. During this time, I will line all of you up at the doors into the auditorium. When I introduce you, you may enter and walk down the aisle to your seats. Now go."

The senior shuffled around the crowded room. Over the next five minutes, they formed two loose lines of people. Maybrook led them out into the hallway, where he spent another several minutes checking the lines against his clipboard. He had to check that everyone was present and in the correct spot.

"Good. Follow me to the lobby." The president turned and guided them to the lobby, where he motioned for the two lines to wait by the two sets of double doors. From the amount of conversation coming through the door, Gus figured the auditorium was nearly full. Being at the front of the second line, he peeked around the corner and scanned the crowd for Art and Neil. He found them, sitting at the far right of the back row.

After a few minutes, the dean of students, a short, thin, balding man by the name of Westford, approached the podium. The room fell silent as he tapped the microphone.

"Good morning. I ask you all to stand and place your hands over your hearts as we recite the Pledge of Allegiance to begin the ceremony." He spoke slowly in a calm, soothing voice.

As they started, Maybrook entered the auditorium and climbed the stairs onto the stage. When Westford finished, he nodded at the president and sat down. Maybrook stepped behind the podium to speak.

"I am the president of this university. My name is Otto Maybrook. I am proud to begin the eighty-second commencement ceremony here at Central Illinois University. I do not wish to waste any of your time, so here are your graduates!"

Maybrook raised his hands and gestured for the seniors to enter the room. The two lines slowly approached the front rows, one person at a time. The crowd cheered continuously as the graduates entered, grinning and waving. The applause faded slowly as the final students took their seats. Suddenly, the room plunged into darkness.

"Everybody remain calm," Maybrook said, speaking loudly. "I am sure our sound and lights crew will resolve this issue shortly."

Suddenly a single spotlight flicked on, illuminating one of the doors into the lobby. As the crowd began to murmur, Gus locked eyes with Mikey. They exchanged a look before turning to see what would unfold.

A loud pop sounded from a few rows behind Gus, startling him. He looked around and noticed a long cylinder jutting into the air. Then he registered something falling around him and held out his hand to catch a piece of confetti.

The confetti cannon was followed by a record scratch over the sound system. The system began to blare festive Hispanic music as cannons popped and spread confetti around the auditorium. Another spotlight powered on, aiming at the other set of doors. Both sets flung open, and Gus busted out in laughter when he saw what was entering the room.

Two groups of men, totaling about a dozen, strolled coolly into the room. Each of them wore a black suit with a brightly colored shirt. They hid their faces with horse masks and finished the out-fit with large sombreros.

Gus glanced over his shoulder to see May-brook's reaction. Fortunately, the person in charge of lights shone a spotlight on him. Think-ing quickly, he pulled out his phone, opened the camera, and took a close-up of Maybrook's ex-pression. Gus looked at his picture and saw the pulsing vein in his forehead.

An eruption of noise called his attention to the group entering the room. Between the dozen men, half of them wielded a pair of maracas, while the others raised vuvuzelas to their lips. As they shimmied up the aisles, they alternated shaking the maracas vigorously and blowing deeply into the horns.

About halfway up the aisles, the visitors began to stop every six feet or so. Once the last one stopped, they suddenly stood upright. They dropped their instruments simultaneously and reached up to grab their costumes in the chest and belt. The music and lights faded.

The room became silent and still for a few sec-onds. Without warning, the music gained volume and immediately jumped to a bass drop. The lights flashed on the figures in the aisles as they tore their mariachi costumes off. Underneath, each man was outfitted in neon, skintight shorts and tank tops.

The crowd roared upon seeing this. Some yelled in disgust, while most of the room shouted excitedly and whistled. Gus doubled over laughing as the lights began to flicker and fade from color to color.

The neon-clad men sprang to life. Some started pelvic-thrusting in place, while the rest ran around the auditorium. The latter group jumped around and thrust their fists into the air. As this commotion spread throughout the room, Gus heard the lobby doors fling open again and turned to face them.

Another dozen men darted into the room, clothed from head to toe in black. They even wore ski masks to conceal their identities. The first three in each group had several cans taped to their torso. They grabbed one in each hand, raised it above their heads, and started shooting silly string all over the audience. When their first cans emptied, they dropped them to the floor and pulled more off their shirts.

While this unfolded, Gus watched the rest of the second group to see what they were doing. They seemed to be empty-handed, but he knew that Donovan would never involve useless people in his pranks. The first group met these new arrivals in the aisles and huddled together. There was movement, but Gus could not see what was happening.

The two huddles separated quickly and moved to the front of the auditorium. They all flung their arms upward, tossing what looked like small, flickering lights into the air. With that, they hurried out of the auditorium through the side doors. Noticing that the silly string group was also gone, Gus stared intently at the tossed lights, trying to identify them.

As Gus realized what the lights were, they exploded. In an instant, the room filled with light and sound. Flashes of white, yellow, red, and blue scattered across the space above the audience. A procession of popping, whizzing, and crackling followed the light. As the commotion died, a thin cloud of smoke settled throughout the room.

Everyone's attention turned to the stage. Maybrook stood motionless behind the podium with his head down. A few moments passed before he did anything. Without a word, he lifted his head, looked at the crowd, and applauded.

"Good job, boys," he said into the microphone. "Thank you for making this ceremony a

... unique experience. Fortunately, I know all of your names, so I will contact you this weekend about this little ... incident. If you have any string or confetti on you, I ask that you simply brush it off so we can continue the commencement. It would take a great deal of time to empty the auditorium, clean up this mess, and bring everyone back. Please take the next few minutes to make yourselves more comfortable."

10

Maybrook paused as the audience began to murmur. Gus saw movement throughout the room as people brushed themselves off or moved seats. The dull commotion slowly died down as everyone's eyes focused on the stage.

"Good morning, friends and family," the president started. "Welcome to the eighty-second commencement ceremony here at Central Illinois University. We have gathered here to honor the students who have worked hard over the last several years and completed all the requirements that we placed before them. These students are your friends, family, and loved ones. You have watched them grow from children into the young adults they are today.

"While they have completed their degrees here at Central Illinois University, they still have a long way to go. It is our hope that their success here motivates them to excel in their futures, whatever they may be. To do that, the student body president will share some parting thoughts with her peers. Ms. Cecilia Domingo has been an outstanding student and leader on this campus. She has served as the student's president for the last two years and managed to graduate *summa cum laude* with a Bachelor's degree in marketing. Now, welcome Ms. Domingo to the podium!"

Maybrook backed away from the podium, clapping slowly. Applause erupted around the room as Cici climbed the stairs to the stage. She wore a red gown for the ceremony, and her long hair framed her face with curls. She pulled a sheet of paper from the podium and cleared her throat.

"Good morning. As President Maybrook said, we are here to graduate!" Cici began cheerfully. "I have loved my years here at CIU, so I couldn't wait to talk to you all today. But I know that all of my peers, myself included, are excited to graduate, so I'll keep this short. I only want to share a single story with you.

"It was the end of my first semester here. I had survived taking twenty-one credit hours up to this point, but the last few assignments were due and finals loomed. I was stressed out of my mind and running on a few hours of sleep, when one night, there was a knock at my door. I ignored it because I had to finish my homework, but the person continued knocking.

"When I answered the door, I saw my RA Charlie standing in front of me, with a small gift bag in her hand. She strolled into my room without any invitation, set the bag on my desk, and claimed my seat in front of my work. For a moment, I simply stood there confused.

"I finally approached her and started to ask why she was here, but she interrupted me. She explained that the RAs have purchased gifts for the freshmen for years to help them relax during finals. She then stopped talking, looked me up and down, and started laughing hysterically.

"I was a hot mess. Half of my hair was in a sloppy bun, my makeup had smeared across my face, and my shirt was inside-out. I probably looked like a raccoon with the massive bags under my eyes.

"I watched her laugh at me for a moment before joining in. Before I knew it, we were both lying on the floor, trying to share stories and jokes and memories as we laughed. I'm not sure how long we lay there, but eventually I fell asleep. Then I woke up a few hours later and re-entered full-panic homework mode.

"Charlie showed up again the next night. And

the next night. And every night until I went home for Christmas. Then, during the spring semester, she would randomly barge into my room at midnight, force me away from my homework, and take me to Wal-Mart or Steak n Shake. Through all of that, Charlie became my first college friend.

"I tell you that to remind you of the lesson that I learned the hard way. You see, I came here with the intention of graduating in three years and diving right into the workforce. I planned to take twenty-one credits a semester and graduate quickly. But Charlie changed my mind. She didn't talk me out of it. In fact, we never talked about my college plan.

"Instead, she loved me out of it. She showed me that people are so much more important than any work you do. Whether you're in high school or college, or if you're a big-wig CEO or a humble janitor, people matter. They are what makes life worth living.

"You can work all day, every day, until you die. But that work won't show up at your funeral. It won't cry over your passing, and it won't share memories of the good ole days. That's why you meet people, make friends, and impact lives. People will be there to celebrate your successes and mourn your failures, but work will never do that.

Work will take your time and energy, but people will give you theirs.

"Look around you, my dear classmates. Remember the professors who taught you, the guys and gals who lived with you, and the friends who took you to Steak n Shake at midnight to eat pancakes and write papers. Without them, college is just a bunch of money, time, and stress spent to get a sheet of paper.

"So I implore all of you to cherish the people in your lives. Love them, and be loved by them. As we leave this place today, always remember that. Measure your life by the people who love you, not by the things you've accomplished. Thank you."

Cici bowed quickly and returned to her seat as the audience applauded. The noise slowly faded as Maybrook returned to the podium. Soon only one person continued to clap.

Gus took a deep breath and stood as he stopped clapping. He bent down, reached under his seat, and removed a bottle of root beer from the underside. The surrounding students followed his lead excitedly, murmuring amongst themselves as they discovered bottles taped under each of their own seats.

"Before we continue," he shouted, turning

slowly to speak to the entire room, "I propose a toast! Professor Maybrook, feel free to join us! I taped a bottle inside the podium just for you." The man's face revealed no emotion as he found and raised his bottle.

"Let us toast in celebration of this day! Congratulations to us all for making it to graduation! Cheers!" Gus yelled, raising his bottle.

"Cheers!" the seniors repeated.

"Cheers," Maybrook agreed. The seniors in the audience clinked bottles with their neighbors. Gus pointed the neck of his bottle towards Maybrook, who smirked and returned the favor. Then, they twisted the tops off the bottles and chugged the liquid inside.

11

"Congratulations!" Gus had barely emerged from the auditorium when his mother Ruby wrapped him in a tight hug. She was a young brunette, wearing a blouse with designer jeans and flats. Her husband, an older, rugged man named Dave, stood nearby.

"Good job son," Dave said, shaking Gus's hand sternly.

"Thanks Mom. Thanks Dave. How did you like the toast?"

"It was great!" Ruby replied. "Unexpected, but it was a pleasant surprise. It's great to see you coming out of your shell and having fun."

"Mom, you think everything I do is great," he retorted, chuckling.

"Because it is! Also, now that you've graduated, when are you going to get married and give me some grandchildren?"

"Honey, couldn't you let him enjoy gradua-tion for a bit before starting that again?" Dave asked teasingly. "Don't worry about it, Gus. You know she's teasing."

"Well, for the most part," Gus agreed. "I *am* her only shot at grandkids!"

"Not if you count me!" Mikey interrupted, putting his arm around Gus's shoulders. "Hey Ruby, hey Dave! Thanks for coming!"

"Mikey!" Ruby exclaimed, hugging him tightly. "Where's your family? And Amber?"

"Um the family is over there talking to Doc," he answered, pointing over his shoulder. "Amber is still in Tennessee. She has some final labs and stuff to finish up this weekend."

"Well you'll have to bring her up to Rockville this summer!" she said. "I miss her!"

"I'll see what I can do! How are you two?"

"Busy," Dave grumbled. "I work this evening, so we need to leave soon. But I'm glad we got to see the two of you graduate. We're proud of you."

"Agreed!" Ruby added, rummaging in her purse. "We'll all have to come back next year for when Neil and Art graduate. Here's some cash for food tonight. Treat yourselves well since it's a special day! Sorry we couldn't stay longer!" She handed a wad of bills to Gus who straightened them and slipped them into his pocket.

"See you guys at home!" he said, hugging Ruby and shaking Dave's hand. They left as Mikey's family surrounded them.

"Hey young man!" Randy Kilroy greeted, patting Gus on the back. He was a stocky man with a receding hairline and a dark goatee, which he stroked absentmindedly.

"Hello Randy," Gus replied. "How was the drive down?"

"It was nice," Mikey's mom Michelle answered. She was a portly woman with short, dark hair dressed in scrubs. "The younger kids were asleep, and Jenny and Suzie were on their phones the whole time. So Randy and I got to enjoy three hours of peace and quiet."

"Have you met all of the kids?" Randy asked. Before Gus could respond, Randy introduced him to Jenny, Suzie, twins Amy and Kim, Caleb, and Tyler. Jenny and Suzie were close to his age, but the others were in elementary school.

"Not going to lie, I probably won't remember all of your names," Gus admitted. "I do know Jenny and Suzie from Facebook though, so I won't forget yours."

"Well we just came by to say hello before we

kidnapped Mikey for the afternoon," Randy explained. "The family doesn't get together very often anymore, so we wanted to take advantage of this time."

"Don't be a stranger this summer, though!" Michelle added, giving Gus a quick hug. "You're welcome to come up anytime! I'm sure Mikey would love that."

"Thanks, Michelle, I'll see what I can do!" As the family started to walk away, Gus and Mikey locked eyes. The latter mouthed, *Help me*, but all Gus could do was shrug apologetically.

"Where's he going?" Art asked, suddenly appearing behind him with Neil.

"Goodness people!" Gus exclaimed. "I'm about to go back to the dorm. I need a nap after all of our shenanigans lately. And to answer your question, his family wants some time with him today. So we're Mikey-less for the afternoon."

"Bummer. What are we going to do all day without him?" Neil asked, untying his tie.

"Um probably the same stuff we do with him," Art said. "Play video games, watch Netflix, and eat junk food."

"Perfect! Let's blow this joint and get to it!" Neil weaved his way through the crowds in the lobby and headed outside. As they left, Gus locked eyes with Maybrook from across the room. The man grinned slightly and nodded at Gus, who offered a small salute in return.

"Drop what you're doing right now!" The boys turned to see Mikey darting into the room, out of breath.

"Why?" Art asked.

"Just come on! Follow me!" Neil shrugged and followed Mikey, with Art and Gus right behind him. "We're going to the roof," Mikey explained as they walked.

"Funny story, guys," Neil began as Gus carded the door. "The last time I was up here, I ran into a couple that I know having sex. As if that wasn't awkward enough, they paused to say hi before going back to their business. Needless to say, I wasn't up here long."

"Let me give you some advice," Mikey responded, leading the way up the stairs. "Don't ever tell that story again." Neil laughed and agreed as they opened the door at the top of the stairs and stepped onto the roof.

The group fell silent as they took in the scene around them. The trees and grass were vibrant green as far as the eye could see. The sky was clear of all clouds, so the setting sun painted it shades of orange, pink, purple, and yellow. These colors glowed around them.

"Shoot dang," Art muttered after a moment.

"I take it this is what you wanted us to see?" Mikey asked.

"Oh yea. I saw it through the bathroom window and figured the view would be better up here," Mikey explained. "Plus, why not end today with a beautiful sunset?"

"Good call," Neil said.

The group fell silent again. Each of the boys pulled out their phones and took photos, trying to capture the moment. Pocketing their phones, they sat down on the edge of the roof, feet dangling three stories above the ground. They sat quietly and the sun sink beneath the horizon. When it finally disappeared, they stood up and started down the stairs back to their room.

"Say what you want about the Midwest," Gus said, "but we have some awesome sunsets here."

12

The next couple of days consisted of Netflix, video games, and junk food. Mikey and Gus had no finals or projects to do, and Neil and Art procrastinated theirs. On Monday night, they ate dinner in the cafeteria. While returning to their dorms, Neil brought up his project.

"I can't hang out tonight," he began. "I have to write my paper."

"What class is it?" Art asked.

"It's for one of my music classes." Neil was studying music business, aspiring to be a producer and musician one day.

"It's due at 8:00 tomorrow morning, right?" Neil nodded, and Mikey jabbed him in the arm. "Maybe you shouldn't have procrastinated until the night before!"

"I mean, I'll get it done," he defended. "I just may not sleep much tonight. Or at all. It's only twelve pages! I'll start when we get back." Neil locked himself in his room while his friends made a Wal-Mart trip and resumed their Netflix binge.

The next morning, Gus found a note on Neil's door as he headed to the shower room: "Wake me up before lunch." He shook his head disappointedly as he continued to the showers.

Returning from his shower, Gus found Mikey and Art both on their laptops in his room. He could tell that they were in the middle of a game of *League*, as their mice clicked constantly. As he dried off, Gus realized something.

"Looks like we're back to our normal routines," he noted aloud. "You guys playing *League* all day with Netflix in the background. Neil procrastinating his homework, then staying up all night to finish it. Then there's me balancing my time between Facebook and video games."

"That reminds me," Mikey added without looking up. "Art, how's studying going?"

"Define 'going,'" he answered. "I'll study in a bit. It's just a psych exam. I actually pay attention and know that stuff because it's my major. It's all of the *other* classes that I don't care about because they won't make me the best counselor ever."

Aside from the periodic shouts from Art and Mikey, conversation died. When lunchtime arrived, Gus grabbed his Nerf gun and carded

Neil's door.

"Hey stupid!" he shouted. "It's almost time for lunch!" Without waiting for him to respond, Gus shot a large red dart at his face. Neil grumbled loudly and rolled out of bed.

"Give me five," he mumbled groggily, pushing Gus out into the hall and shutting the door. He emerged a couple of minutes later, dressed and holding a can of Mountain Dew.

After lunch, Art went to take his final. Gus wandered campus with Neil and Mikey. They meandered through every building and classroom, reminiscing on the various memories and lessons from their time at college. When they returned to their rooms, Art was already there and in the middle of a game of *League*.

"How'd your exam go?" Gus asked as they all sat down.

"Well I didn't fail," he replied, laughing. "I think I got about a C on it." When he finished his current game, he started playing *Call of Duty* with the group. Gus participated this time, even though he was terrible at first-person shooters.

The next day arrived quickly. The guys all woke up early to clean, pack, and rearrange their rooms. Neil moved a portable speaker into the hallway and blared Japanese pop music as they cleaned. Throughout the ordeal, they randomly stopped to sing and dance ridiculously, even though they did not understand the song lyrics.

By noon, their rooms were back in order. Furniture was returned to its original position, and everyone's belongings filled various boxes and bags. Art received a call from his parents telling him that they were on campus, so they got ready to carry things outside.

"I'm probably going to leave too," Neil admitted. "I have a three-hour drive ahead of me. Plus putting off this whole 'goodbye' thing is miserable." Between the four of them, they managed to gather all of Neil and Art's things in a single trip and carry them to the parking lot. As Neil headed to pull his car up, Gus helped Art load his things into his parents' car.

When both vehicles were loaded, the guys stood in the middle of the parking lot. There was an awkward silence as they looked from one person to the next. Gus cleared his throat.

"Well, this is it," he started. "Time for you guys to start summer vacation. Time for Mikey and me to spend our last night on campus."

"But this isn't goodbye!" Neil interrupted. "Wherever you guys go, we'll come visit!"

"And we'll make sure we come back and hang

out!" Mikey assured them.

"Plus we have texting and Facebook," Art added. "We'll stay in touch!"

"Exactly!" Gus agreed. "So this isn't goodbye. It's just 'see you later.'"

"Group hug!" Neil yelled, pulling Art and Mikey into a half bear hug. Gus joined, and they all stood there in a huddle for a moment before stepping away.

"All right, time to go," Art said. The four quickly exchanged fist bumps and bro-hugs.

Mikey and Gus started walking toward the dorm, while their roommates headed to their respective vehicles. Gus was the first to stop, turn around, and yell, "See you guys!" Neil and Art immediately returned the sentiment.

As the cars drove away, Gus became aware of a heaviness in his chest and stomach. "I know this goodbye is only temporary," he mumbled, "but that doesn't make it suck any less."

13

Gus and Mikey spent some time packing silently before sitting down to watch Vine compilations and anime parodies. Aside from quoting their favorite lines, the pair remained silent.

When the next morning dawned, they packed the last of their belongings and hauled them to their respective cars. They shut the doors to their barren rooms and stood in the hallway, staring at the floor. They waited in silence for a while.

"Well," Mikey said, breaking the silence, "this is really it. The moment we've waited for: the moment when we leave CIU once and for all."

"I can't believe how quickly these four years flew," Gus muttered. "It feels like we moved in just a few weeks ago, but now we're leaving."

"Yea, I hear you. So much has happened over the years. We've been through some of the best and worst times together. In a way, it seems like all of that didn't matter, like it's just ending here."

"In a way, it is. Those moments are behind us, and now our setting is changing. We're moving into the next act of our lives."

"Let's get this over with." Mikey inhaled deeply. "Last one to their car buys the group B Dubs when we get together again?"

"Deal!" Gus agreed. "On three."

"One…two…three…go!" Gus took off toward the back door, while Mikey sprinted the other direction down the hallway.

Bounding out the door, Gus turned toward the parking lot and ran. As he came around the front of the dorm, he saw Mikey throw the front doors open and continue down the sidewalk. Gus picked up his pace, refusing to lose. He reached his car a moment later, threw the driver's door open, and collapsed in the seat. As he shut the door, Gus caught his breath and pulled out his cell phone to text Mikey.

"Clever girl," he typed. "Now we don't know who won. I'll buy B Dubs."

"Manchester! I'll tell Art and Neil!"

"Fine, whatever. Now get outta here. We have long drives ahead of us."

Gus started the car and fastened his seat belt. He glanced in the rearview to back out of his spot when a familiar SUV flew past him and honked.

His phone vibrated, alerting him to a new message: "See you soon, bro."

Tossing his phone aside, Gus backed out of the parking spot and drove off.

Barren cornfields gave way to the rural town of Rockville. Gus drove through town, passing a few businesses and a couple of small neighborhoods. As he stopped at a red light, he returned waves to the drivers that crossed the intersection. The light changed to green, and the road quickly gave way to more barren cornfields.

Leaving town, Gus left the highway and weaved his way down dirt roads until he found his house. It was a gray one-story building set back from the road. Woods surrounded it on three sides, with a long driveway dividing the front lawn. Gus pulled up to the house and parked next to his mom's car. He noticed his stepdad's truck parked in the lawn beside the house. Opening his door, a large black shape immediately jumped into his lap.

"Hey Benji," Gus grunted, petting the lab. Benji's tail whipped back and forth, thudding against the side of the car, as he stretched to lick Gus's face.

"Okay, down boy." Gus pushed the dog away and stood up. Grabbing his backpack from the passenger seat, he shut the door and walked into his house. He kicked off his shoes in the foyer and walked into the kitchen, where his mom was putting away groceries.

"Gus!" she exclaimed, turning to face him.

"Hey Mom," he answered, hugging her. Setting his backpack on the floor, he helped her put away groceries as they talked.

"How was the drive?"

"It was fairly uneventful. Not much traffic. It was a little sad; the radio couldn't seem to stop playing sad songs."

"That stinks. Did you enjoy your last week with the guys?"

"It was perfect. Just us doing what we do best: staying up way too late watching Netflix, playing video games, and eating junk food! Neil and Art left yesterday, so Mikey and I had one last night to hang out before we parted ways."

"Speaking of, how are the guys? Dave and I didn't get to see them when we were there for graduation."

"Art and Neil are the same. Lots of shenanigans, not a lot of homework. Mikey isn't too excited about going home, but I'm sure he'll find something to get him out of the house."

"He's always welcome here," Ruby said. "Especially if he brings Amber!"

"I'll let him know. I'm sure he'll come visit sometime this summer. Maybe I can get Art and Neil here too, so you'll have a houseful!"

"That sounds good! Have them all come over at the end of the summer. I'll cook a ton of food for you!" Putting away the last of the groceries, Gus's mom left the kitchen.

"Okay, I'll talk to them!" he yelled after her. Gus picked up his backpack and went to his room, which was off the kitchen. He dropped his backpack on his desk and headed outside to start bringing his belongings inside.

Several trips later, boxes cluttered his room. His bedding sat in a pile in the corner, next to his clothes hamper. He took the hamper to the laundry room to wash his clothes. On the way back, he grabbed a bowl of sour cream and onion chips and a bottle of Dr. Pepper from the kitchen. Back in his room, Gus's phone buzzed.

"Hey," he answered, popping a few chips into his mouth.

"How was the drive?" Mikey asked. Gus could hear commotion in the background.

"Pretty bland. I just drove quickly and tried

not to think about much of anything."

"Same. My freaking parents left as soon as I pulled into the driveway. Now I'm stuck babysitting the kids."

"Are Jenny or Suzie back from school yet?"

"Jenny has finals next week, so she'll be home in about a week. Suzie is probably at a friend's house. So no, it's just me for now."

"That sucks. I just got done hauling my stuff inside. I helped Mom put away groceries when I first got home."

"How is Mom?"

"She's good. She loves her work, but it keeps her busy a lot. She also misses all of you guys, since she had to leave right after graduation. She said you all can come visit before summer ends. But only if you bring Amber."

Mikey chuckled. "I'll see what I can do. We should message Art and Neil and see when they're free. Maybe we all can take a few days, or even a week, and just come hang."

"That would be legit! Mom said she'd cook for you guys!"

"Oh dang! I guess I'm moving into your place for the summer!" Mikey joked. "I'll talk to Amber while I'm down there this weekend and see if she can take some time away from her mom's salon and come visit."

"Good! Is she ready to graduate?"

"Oh yea! She actually interviewed with a hospital last week. If she didn't hear back already, they should call her tomorrow."

"That's awesome! So is she going to move in with her relatives down there?"

"That's the current plan." Mikey paused to tell the kids to stop jumping on the furniture. "She'll start working, and her family offered to help me find an apartment and a job. They'll even open up their couch for me to crash there."

"Awesome! Sounds like you have a plan!"

"Yep! I'll move down there sometime this summer. I have some things to do up here first, though. Like not kill my parents. Anyway, I'll let you go. I know I need to unpack a bit, so you surely do too. Tell Mom that I'll text her and find a time to visit! See you bro."

"Okay, see you bro." Gus hung up the phone and sat down on his bed. As he snacked on his chips, someone knocked on the door. It opened, and his mom stuck her head into the room.

"Was that Mikey?" she asked.

"Yea. He says that he'll text you and talk about coming down for a few days. He'll see Amber tomorrow, so they'll see if she has time to visit."

"Good! I can't wait!" She glanced at the various boxes scattered across the floor. "Are you going to unpack?"

"I don't think so," Gus said, sighing. "I'll probably just sort through everything. Decide what I'll take with me wherever I go after the summer, trash or give away the rest."

"That's fine. Let me know if you need a hand. I wanted to let you know that I'm going to bed. I have to be at work at 6." She crossed the room and hugged him.

"Night Mom. I'll talk to you more tomorrow."

"Good night." She shut the door on her way out. Gus plopped onto his bed, lying on his back and staring out the window. He watched the branches sway in the wind until he drifted off.

14

A few days later, Ruby brought home Chinese for dinner. She set the boxes on the dining room table while Gus grabbed plates and a couple of forks. Sitting down, his mom went to the back of the house to get his stepdad from his office.

"Hey Gus," he said, coming into the room.

"Hey Dave. What have you been doing: farming or milling?"

"Farming," he answered, sitting down. "The neighbors have been planting corn and beans lately. I think they need my hands this week, then I'll be back at the mill full-time until the middle of June. Then detassling starts."

As he spoke, Ruby opened the boxes of chicken, rice, and steamed vegetables. She always got sweet n sour and teriyaki chicken and brown and white rice. She passed out chopsticks to the two guys. She grabbed soy sauce from the pantry and set it on the table.

"Let's eat!" she declared, taking her seat. They dumped mounds of food onto their plates. Ruby picked up her chopsticks and started to eat.

"Mom, you know we don't use chopsticks," Gus joked. "There's only one way that we can use them." He clenched one in his fist and, in one swift motion, jabbed it through a large piece of chicken. He proceeded to bite the meat off the stick, having made a shish kebab.

"So Gus," Dave began through a mouthful of rice, "what are your plans for the summer? And for after it?"

"Well I can help you out with detassling when that starts. I can either do it or supervise and teach the high schoolers how to do it. Otherwise I'll figure it out as I go. I talked to Dr. J last week about my options. We didn't really land anywhere specific, but he gave me a couple of ideas of where to start. I've been doing research into graduate schools and degrees."

"What have you found?" Dave asked.

"I talked with the guys a bit. Mikey told me about Doc's suggestion of abnormal psych. That would give me opportunities to counsel individuals, particularly those with special needs. Kyle from high school is a teacher, so he and I discussed that option. That would limit me to the state in which I receive a license, but I would have constant access to kids to teach and help. The other big thought in my head is social work. I could counsel or teach with it, as well as facilitate policy change to benefit."

"Which seems to be the best fit for what you want to do?"

"Well there are pros and cons to each," Gus began. "For example, psychology would probably take the most time. I'd need to take some undergrad psych classes before I could even apply. Teaching would limit me to a specific state and area of focus. And social work is such a broad field that I would need to specialize."

"Oh don't be so negative," Ruby interrupted. "What are some of the positives?"

"Well, psychology would primarily be one-on-one encounters, which are often more meaningful in the long run. Teaching provides a context for countless interactions and opportunities to teach. I learned a lot about life from my high school teachers. And social work can include any number of different experiences, from counseling to Social Service work to policy development. So it would let me do almost anything."

"Hmm," Dave grunted. "At least you've put some thought into it. Have you applied to check if you can get in anywhere?"

"Not yet," Gus answered. "I texted Dr. J to catch him up on my research so far. He hasn't responded with any further advice or direction. I do have a few places in mind to consider pursuing a Master's though, don't worry."

"Very good!" Ruby chimed. "Anyway, how are the guys? Mikey and Amber?"

"They're good," Gus answered, scooping some vegetables into his mouth. "Amber graduated this weekend, so Mikey was down there. He plans to move later this summer and look for a job and a place to live. Art went back home to do nothing all summer, and Neil probably started at the sub shop where he worked last summer."

"I'm thinking of having them all over for a few days," his mom added. "I haven't seen them since October, and I'd like to see Mikey before he grows up and gets too busy for us."

"Hm. Any idea when that will happen?"

"I'll let you know, honey." She smiled and popped a piece of broccoli into her mouth.

"It would be good to have Mikey around again. I could use an extra pair of hands to look at the neighbors' tractors. And our cars too, while he's at it. If only he'd move back in and help keep the house and property in order." Dave looked at

Gus and chuckled.

"I'm sure he'd love to help, and he's much more proficient than me!" Gus said. "He loves being here, and he enjoys that kind of work. If not for Amber in Tennessee, he would probably just take over my room once I leave!"

Conversation diminished as they each poured seconds onto their plates. As they finished their last bites, Ruby reached into her purse and pulled out three fortune cookies. She handed one to Dave and one to Gus.

"Open on the count of three," she instructed. "1...2...3!" They all cracked their cookies in half, pulled out their fortunes, and read them.

"'Open your mind and your heart to good things.' Well, based on the conversation we just had, I should keep an open mind about Gus's plans for the summer. Whatever you do, son, I'm sure it will benefit you in some way." Dave looked at Gus as he said this. Feeling awkward, he simply stared at his cookie and nodded.

Gus's mom went next. "'Your home will be filled with peace and harmony.' My cookie must mean that Mikey and Amber will visit soon! That's the only explanation!" She laughed and popped a piece of her cookie in her mouth.

"'Work with what you have,'" Gus read. "I

guess I could skip graduate school and just work with the Bachelor's degree that I currently have!" Dave glared at him skeptically across the table. "Kidding, kidding!" he replied, waving his arms in front of him.

They all laughed and stood up from the table. Clearing off the trash and dishes, Gus returned to his room. He crawled into his bed and picked up *The Hitchhiker's Guide to the Galaxy* to continue reading. Over the next few days, he spent his time reading and sorting through his belongings. By the middle of the week, he had a large pile of possessions that he no longer wanted.

Gus loaded the pile into his car and drove to Terre Haute. He dropped everything off at the Salvation Army there and headed back home. As he turned into the driveway, he saw that an SUV had parked in his mom's spot. He pulled up next to it, shut off the engine, and realized that he recognized the vehicle.

"Hey Gus!" Mikey stepped out the front door, and Benji charged at him. He knelt to pet the dog as Gus approached him.

"Why are you here?"

"Mom invited me, dummy," he replied, not looking up from Benji.

"I guess she forgot to tell me," Gus muttered.

"Unless—"

"She wanted to surprise you," Mikey interrupted. "She told me to come up around the middle of the week because she was going to take the day off."

"Then where is she? She got up and left early like she does when she works."

"You'll see." Without another word, Mikey turned and went back into the house. Gus followed and discovered Art and Neil sitting in the living room.

"You guys are here too?" Art and Neil jumped up to give him a group hug.

"Yep. Mikey picked Art up, then they crashed at my place last night," Neil explained. "Art and I wanted to make plans to visit you, so when Mikey called us last week, we dropped everything to make this trip happen."

"I'm sure there wasn't much to drop," Gus remarked, smirking. "Well, since you're all here, how about some lunch? We have plenty of food. What do you guys want?"

"Surprise us!" Art said. "Do you mind if we hook up the PlayStation in the living room?"

"Um we don't believe in PlayStation in this house." Gus went to the freezer and began looking through the shelves.

Finding a large bag of Pizza Rolls, Gus spread them on a pair of cookie sheets and stuck them in the oven. He set the kitchen timer, grabbed four cans of Mountain Dew from the fridge, and went to the living room. Passing out the drinks, he sat on the floor and leaned against the couch as Art and Mikey played *Call of Duty*.

The boys took turns playing and snacked on Pizza Rolls and chips all afternoon. Around four o'clock, Ruby returned with a couple of grocery bags. She set them on the counter and entered the living room to greet Mikey and the others.

"Hey guys!" she exclaimed, hugging them all in turn. "How was the drive?"

"Not too bad," Mikey answered. "We stayed at Neil's outside West Lafayette last night, so it wasn't even a two-hour drive."

"That's good. You guys bring your appetite? I'm making steaks!" With a smile, she went to her room and came back wearing yoga pants and a plain white shirt. She pulled her hair into a bun and returned to the kitchen.

"Do you want a hand?" Gus offered, standing up from the couch.

"No, you enjoy having your friends here!" his mom replied. "I'll let you all know when it's ready." The sounds and smells of cooking gradually filled the air.

When his mom turned on the electric mixer, Gus left the living room and started setting the table. He grabbed six plates, cloth napkins, and sets of silverware and spread them across the table. He began placing the food on the table as his mom finished mixing the potatoes and brought them over. Gus and his friends claimed their seats as Ruby went to get Dave.

"Dig in, boys!" Dave announced, taking his seat. They passed food around until everyone had filled their plates with sirloin steak, mashed potatoes, green beans, and rolls. They started eating without another word.

"This is wonderful!" Mikey exclaimed, mouth full. "I didn't realize how much I missed good, home-cooked food until just now!" Art and Neil voiced their agreement through grunts as they stuffed more food into their mouths.

"How's Miss Amber doing?" Ruby asked, looking at Mikey.

"Ugh," Gus groaned, rolling his eyes. "With how much I've heard that question, I might as well be engaged to her myself!"

"Not my fault we know the same people and they all love Amber!" Mikey retorted. "She's good! She graduated last weekend, so I was down there to see her. She heard back from an interview she had, and she got the job! She's had training and stuff all week."

"What's she doing there?"

"She'll be a pediatric nurse. Basically, she runs around the children's wing of the hospital and take care of the sick kiddos."

"That's cool!" Ruby replied. "Where is this hospital?"

"It's in Nashville," Mikey said. "She has family who live there, so she's going to live with them for now. I plan to move down there sometime next month to find a place to live. I've done some job searching, and I lined up some interviews for the end of June. With some help from Doc."

"That's what Gus said," Dave interjected. "If only he could figure his life out as much as you have." Both Dave and Gus chuckled.

"Yea, he really is the most irresponsible of our group," Mikey teased. "I've been trying to help him grow up for four years, but clearly it hasn't worked!" He gave Gus a playful jab and stole a roll from his plate.

"I mean," Gus defended, "I already said I'd help with detassling. And I have plenty of mail from universities across the country, offering me scholarships to attend grad school."

"Boo, grad school!" Neil exclaimed between bites. "Grad school is for nerds!"

"Well thankfully none of us are nerds," Art added sarcastically. "This is what you two get for graduating and becoming adults, you mooks."

"Says the one who took Written Comp three times," Mikey retorted. "At the rate you two are going, our kids will finish college before you!"

"Whoa now," Neil said, "that was rude. We're simply taking our time. Nobody ever said we had to finish our degrees in four years. We'll get there, one or two passed classes at a time. Adulthood is a patient mistress."

"You," Gus stammered, shaking his head, "you can be such an idiot."

"Oh I know. It doesn't bother me. At least I'm not a boring idiot, right?" Art, Mikey, and Gus awkwardly glanced at each other without responding. "I hate all of you!" Neil tore chunks off a roll and tossed them at each of his friends.

"Whoa now, don't go starting another food fight!" Mikey interrupted as he ate the chunk thrown at him. "Especially here at Mom's house!"

"Yea," Art agreed. "At least wait until we're somewhere public! Or at your place!"

"I'll just save the rest of my plate to surprise

you later," Neil mumbled. He pushed his plate away and leaned backward in his chair to stretch.

"On that note, I propose dessert and drinks!" Ruby declared, getting up from the table. When she returned, she brought an Oreo cream pie and new plates. As she divided the pie equally amongst them all, Dave left the table and came back with a six-pack of beer.

"Consider this a little graduation gift," he said, passing them out. The guys popped off the bottle caps and sipped on their drinks.

When they finished their desserts, Mikey and Neil plopped down on the couch while Art and Gus helped clear the table. Ruby and Dave shooed them out of the kitchen, so they joined their friends in finding a film to watch on Netflix.

"Good night boys," Ruby said when the cleaning was finished. She and Dave retreated to their room to sleep. The boys followed their lead after their film ended.

"Psst, Gus, wake up!" someone whispered, smacking his face gently. He rolled over groggily to locate the speaker and found Mikey, crouching by his bed.

"What the—" he began, but Mikey clapped

his hand over Gus's mouth before he could finish. He narrowed his eyes in confusion, hoping for an explanation.

"Just be quiet," Mikey whispered. "We need you to pack. Bring about a week's worth of clothes and all the money you have. I'm going to remove my hand, so get ready and don't ask any questions."

"What are you talking about?" Gus rubbed his eyes, and as they adjusted to the dark, he saw Art and Neil standing behind Mikey, fully clothed.

"What did I just say? Here are your glasses, now get dressed! We have plans!" Gus sat up in bed and looked at Mikey.

"Come on, dude! Let's have some fun," Neil urged quietly. Suddenly Jameson's secret of life came back to Gus: *live actively, not vicariously*.

"Okay, give me a second," Gus agreed.

"Good," Mikey said. "Because we're going on the biggest adventure of your life."

15

Mikey, Art, and Neil left the room as Gus rolled out of bed. Throwing on the clothes from the day before, he grabbed the suitcase from his closet and began digging through his dresser. He neatly removed and packed half a dozen pairs of jeans and a dozen graphic tees. Gus stuffed all of his socks and boxers into the suitcase, tossed in a Ziploc bag with his toiletries, and zipped it up. He then found his backpack and filled it with his phone charger, a couple of books, and a hoodie. Slipping on his Vans, he grabbed both bags and headed outside.

"About time!" Neil taunted, sitting in the backseat of Mikey's SUV. The trunk was open, and Mikey seemed to be rearranging its contents.

"Here's my suitcase." Gus hoisted it into the back with the others' suitcases. Mikey arranged the suitcases around a large cooler.

"Alright, we're good to go!" Mikey shut the

back quietly and climbed into the driver's seat. Art and Neil had already claimed the backseat, so Gus rode shotgun. Before long, Mikey turned onto the highway.

"Okay, I have to ask," Gus said, rubbing his eyes. "Why in the world did you guys wake me up at 4:00 in the morning for some adventure? Couldn't this have waited until, oh I don't know, a more reasonable hour?" He turned and looked back and forth between his friends.

"Because we wanted to make it more adventurous!" Neil explained. "Why shouldn't we start our amazing road trip adventure with sneaking out of your house?"

"That reminds me!" Gus pulled his phone from his pocket. "I should let Mom know where I'm going."

"Don't worry about it," Mikey interrupted. "This was her idea. I mentioned wanting to take a road trip with you guys, and she told me to go ahead. She didn't want you to spend your summer updating your resume, interviewing for jobs, applying for grad school, and working with Dave. She wanted you to have some fun. It is your last real summer, after all."

"Then he called Neil and me to invite us," Art added. He did not look up from his Vita as he spoke. "So we both packed our bags, grabbed all the money we could, and freed our schedules for a road trip."

"So how long will this trip take?"

"No idea!" Neil answered.

"We're just going to adventure until we're done," Mikey elaborated. "We'll drive around, crash in hotels, and take turns picking places to visit. Maybe it'll last a week, maybe a month, maybe all summer. But we'll have a good time."

"So who picks...first?" Gus barely had time to finish the question when all three of his friends turned and stared at him. "Okay, fine. Give me some time to think."

"Good, because we need gas. Where's the nearest gas station?"

"The Tiki Hut up ahead, on the right. You can't miss it." As conversation died, Mikey turned up the radio, and Gus began searching for nearby places for them to visit. Before long, they could see the glowing light of a gas station.

"Mikey, we need snacks and drinks," Neil said. "You can't have a road trip without lots of junk food and pop!"

"Well I need to pump gas, so you guys figure that stuff out," Mikey replied. "Just remember to grab *some* substantial food, not just junk."

Suddenly getting an idea, Gus turned around to look at Art. "*Paper Towns*?"

"Oh yes!" Art yelled, throwing his Vita into the seat beside him. "We have to do that! I'll buy this round if we do!"

"Do what?" Neil asked.

"It's simple: we just run in there and grab the snacks," Art explained. "We do it all as fast as possible. In the book, they had six minutes to gas up, grab snacks, and go. So we'll divide what we need into three groups, then each of us will be responsible for one."

"I got this," Gus interrupted. "I'll take the substantial food. Neil, you grab snacks. Art, you're on drink duty. Make sure to grab some water too. Good thing this place is empty this early in the morning." As they pulled into the gas station, Gus saw the lone attendant through the window. He read a magazine absentmindedly.

Mikey had yet to stop his SUV fully when the other three unbuckled their seatbelts, threw the doors open, and sprinted to the door. The attendant jumped at the sudden commotion but quickly started laughing as the chaos unfolded in the store. Neil weaved through the aisles, scooping up various packages of candy, cookies, and chips. Art headed to the back of the store and started hauling twelve-packs of pop to the counter. Gus ran along the refrigerator and pulled out handfuls of Lunchables and deli sandwiches. The attendant scanned items as the boys brought them to the counter and stuffed them into plastic bags. While Art grabbed bottles of water, Gus noticed several slices of breakfast pizza in a case by the fountain and grabbed them.

"Will this be all for you?" the attendant asked.

"Yea, that's good," Gus answered, chuckling. The three of them panted lightly as the attendant finished bagging their items.

"What are you guys doing?" He took Art's money and opened the register drawer.

"Road trip," Neil panted. "Just a spontaneous road trip since Gus here just graduated. And so did the guy pumping gas. It was actually his idea." Neil patted him on the shoulder as Art grabbed his change.

As they picked up their various bags, Gus glanced at the brochure rack next to the register. It was primarily full of road maps for the county and the state, but he noticed a brochure for a local attraction. Without a thought, he picked it up, tucked it into his back pocket, and helped Art and Neil haul their purchase to the SUV.

A few minutes later, they had filled the cooler

with water and pop and surrounded it with the various bags of snacks. As they climbed into the car, Gus remembered pulled out the brochure.

"I found us a place to go," he said, holding it up for the guys to see. The front had a picture of a waterfall, with the words "Cataract Falls" in bold above it.

16

A few hours later, they entered the park and stopped the car in the designated parking area. Map in hand, they stepped out and started wandering around the park. Neil read about the park from the brochure.

"Apparently Cataract Falls is the largest waterfall in Indiana," he began. "The upper falls plunge 20 feet, and the lower falls drop 18. Overall, the two falls create a drop of 86 feet!"

"That's pretty intense," Mikey noted. "If only it was just one waterfall. That would be so much more insane!"

"Yeah, if only Indiana was known for waterfalls instead of corn," Gus joked. "It's weird that I've never been here, even though I grew up just a couple of hours away."

"Had you heard of it before you found the brochure?" Neil asked.

"Yea, I know plenty of people from high

school who came here to hike and camp and have picnics."

"What about jumping off the falls?"

"Well, I'm sure people did that, but most of my classmates would jump off the bridge into the lake," Gus explained. "It was so much closer."

"That makes sense," Art murmured. "What else did you do for fun in Rockville?"

"Um nothing. We'd go to Terre Haute or Avon for anything aside from camping or hiking. But Bridge Fest was always fun. People watching and eating lots of delicious food."

"Oh I remember coming down for that!" Art exclaimed. "That was easily one of the best fall breaks I've ever had."

"Did you ever jump off the bridge, Gus?" Mikey asked.

"My guess is not," Neil added.

"Well, uh," Gus stammered, "he's right. I never did. I also didn't learn to swim until last summer, so I would've drowned. But I preferred boating, tubing, and night swimming on the lake, not free-falling into it."

"Well I know what we're doing!" Mikey cheered. "What do you say, Gus?"

"Do I really have a choice? I'm game. I'll jump off the falls."

"Manchester!" Art shouted, laughing diabolically. "Now you have to jump!" He rubbed his hands together menacingly and smirked at Gus.

"Well, I have every intention of jumping," Gus retorted dryly. "And when I do, I hope your pretty little face is ready for my left hand. Or maybe my right. I guess you'll find out."

"I would take a slap to witness that!" Neil added. "So, which one should we do first: the upper or lower falls?"

"Well I can't jump," Art mumbled. "The water would ruin my pump." He motioned to his insulin pump, dangling from his belt loop.

"Dude, just take it off for a bit," Neil replied. "Then you can jump, dry off, and put it back on. You don't even have to do both falls."

"One problem," Gus added. "I didn't bring any swimming trunks or towels."

"Forget the trunks! We'll just jump in our boxers. Our clothes will dry. Plus, my SUV has leather seats, so water won't ruin them." Mikey turned around and locked eyes with Gus, backpedaling slowly as the group walked. "So, you're the brains. Which one first?"

Gus sighed and shook his head. "Well, we parked near the upper falls. So it makes more sense to keep walking, jump off the lower falls, then hurry back to jump off the upper ones."

"Sounds good to me. That's what we'll do!" Grabbing the map from Neil, Mikey led the boys down the path.

After a while, they reached the falls. They stopped and stared at the scene before them. Water cascaded over the rocks, creating white foam where it entered the pool beneath it. Gus had seen a picture of it in the brochure, but the real scene was much more impressive.

"Let's do this," Mikey said, taking off his shirt. Gus glanced around and saw that they were alone. The park had just opened, so it seemed that not many others had arrived.

"I'm going to sit this one out," Art said. "I'll jump the upper falls."

"Manchester!" Gus shouted. "Now we're even. So, unless you want two slaps, you'd better jump the upper falls!"

Art paused and narrowed his eyes at Gus. "I hate you sometimes, you know that?"

"Of course. That's why we lived together for three years."

Gus, Mikey, and Neil stripped to their boxers and trekked to the top of the falls. The water rushed around their legs, so they walked carefully as they approached the edge. The guys played rock-paper-scissors to decide who went first. Gus was the first to lose, so he had to go first. Sighing, he took a few steps back.

"Here goes nothing!" He ran forward and leapt off the falls. "Woohoo!"

Suddenly he plunged into the cold water. As he swam to the surface, he felt a couple more splashes around him. He surfaced, and Neil and Mikey soon joined him above water. They all breathed heavily and shivered.

"Let's not tell Art how cold this water is," Mikey stammered through chattering teeth. Nodding in agreement, they swam back to the bank and stumbled up to where Art waited. They did their best to brush off the water before slipping back into their clothes.

"How was the water?" Art asked.

"It was fine," Mikey lied. The warm May air and bright sun warmed them up quickly as they walked, helping them to stop shivering.

"I took pictures of each of you jumping and sent them to the group."

"Sweet!" Gus checked his phone. He found various pictures of each of them running, jumping, and falling into the water in a group message on Facebook. Chuckling to himself, he saved the best ones to his phone and returned it to Art's messenger bag. "Good thing you never go any-where without that. Otherwise our phones would be ruined."

"To the upper falls?" Neil asked. He started walking along Mill Creek.

It took another half an hour for them to reach the upper falls, and the area was far more populated than when they first arrived. They decided to get some food from the car and have a small picnic while they waited for the crowd to leave. After their picnic, they walked down to the edge of the water and started skipping rocks.

"These people need to leave," Gus grumbled, tossing a rock. Instead of skipping, it splashed into the water and sank.

"I mean, we could just jump," Art suggested. "What's the worst that could happen?"

"Conservation officers tend not to like people swimming in parks and recreation areas," Mikey explained. "I'm not sure how they'd feel about us jumping off the falls."

"Plus I'm pretty sure running around in our boxers might be considered 'public indecency,'" Gus added.

"Don't be such a worrywart," Neil retorted. "We'll give it another hour. Then we're jumping, no matter what."

Agreeing to that, they settled into the wait. Gus grabbed his deck of Superfight cards from his backpack, and they passed the time playing the game. When the hour ended, Mikey detoured to his vehicle while the other two met up with Art. Mikey jogged over to them.

"You guys ready?" Mikey asked, stopping next to them. Shouting in agreement, they kicked off their shoes and took off their shirts. After Art disconnected his pump from his abdomen, they slid off their jeans and ran to the water.

"Just jump!" Neil yelled. Without a word, the four of them leapt off the falls and yelled excitedly as they plunged into the water. When they surfaced, they tried to catch their breath between laughing and coughing.

"Holy frig!" Art cried. "Why didn't you tell me that the water was ice cold?" He splashed water at his friends' faces angrily. He continued flailing and screaming dramatically.

"Because we knew your reaction would be funny!" Gus answered, laughing. "But as funny as it was, let's go. This water is too cold!" As they swam back to shore, they became aware of people shouting at them.

"Judging from the sound of it," Mikey panted, "some people aren't too happy about us going for a swim."

"I don't think it's the swimming that bothers them," Neil said between breaths.

"Oh well. What are they going to do, kick us out?" Mikey teased. "We're leaving anyway. Let's go!"

Climbing out of the water, they hurried to grab their clothes from under the tree. They continued to the car. Taking their seats, they noticed towels spread across the seats. Mikey started the engine and chuckled.

"I figured we'd have to make a quick getaway, so I put these towels down before we jumped." He backed out of their spot and sped out of the park. They found a backroad and pulled over to dry off and get dressed.

"Good job jumping off the falls, Art," Gus said, turning to his roommate.

"Same to you!" he agreed. "High five?" Gus and Art stepped forward and high-fived, before patting each other on the cheek.

"So what's next on the agenda?" Neil asked. "Is there anything we want to do, or are we just gonna find a hotel and crash for the night?"

"Yes," Art replied slowly. "We're going to do all the things, including finding a hotel."

"Well I guess that's settled," Mikey said sarcastically. He climbed into the vehicle and searched on his phone for a nearby hotel. "Apparently there's a Motel 6 in a place called Cloverdale. That's as good of a place as any for a night or two. We can check in and go from there."

"Works for me," Gus replied. "So who gets to pick the next adventure?"

"Neil? Want to take it?" Mikey asked, glancing at him in the rearview mirror. "Art and I are both Illinois natives, so we don't know anything around here."

"Sure, I'll do it," he agreed. "Let me text Matt and see if he has any ideas."

"I'm sure he has *plenty* of ideas," Art replied.

"But how many of them will be *legal*? Or safe?" Gus added, chuckling.

"Guys, you make it sound like my brother is the worst." They paused and stared at him. "You're right, he's kind of a terrible person. But I'm sure his ideas would be a lot of fun."

They continued driving, jamming out to the radio. After a short while, Neil busted out laughing randomly. He leaned forward and whispered something into Mikey's ear, causing him to chuckle.

"That's a pretty good idea," he said. "We're

doing that."

"What are we doing?" Gus asked.

"It'll be a surprise," Neil teased. "But trust me, you've never done this. In fact, I'm confident that you've never even been to the place we'll go."

Gus sighed. "Fine, surprise me. I'm not even going to try to figure it out." He returned his attention to the music, patting out the beat on his knees as he sang along.

When they arrived at the motel, Mikey parked the car and went to rent a room. He came back with a key and led the group to their room with their belongings. They settled in for a night of video games, Netflix, and snacking.

The next morning, Mikey explained that their next destination was in Indianapolis. He refused to offer any more details, so they loaded into the SUV and hit the road. When they arrived in the capital a couple of hours later, they found a motel and checked in.

"This is as good as any other," Neil said, getting out of the car. "We'll be here for a few days. I need to make some arrangements with Matt."

Without another word, they settled into their new room. Over the next couple of days, Neil and

Mikey disappeared every night for several hours. Neil always left fifteen minutes after Mikey, but Gus found it suspicious the first night. Mikey tried playing it off by saying he was calling Amber, while Neil allegedly wanted fresh air. On the subsequent nights, Gus and Art began speculating where they went.

"There are plenty of gay bars that aren't too far away," Art guessed, looking at his phone. "I bet they've been checking those out, trying to find the best one in Indianapolis. But they obviously aren't drinking much, because we'd notice that. But I'm sure they've gotten some phone numbers. Especially Neil, since he lives fairly close."

"They probably got in touch with some contact of Matt's. A drug dealer. So they met him when we first came into town, and now they're doing some odd jobs for the dude so that he'll sell them weed. They spend their nights tracking down thugs and either beating the tar out of them or dropping off product."

"Mikey initially left to call Amber, like he said. But as he left the parking lot, a hooker approached him and offered a two-for-one deal. He texted Neil to invite him along because he's the most likely among us to be interested in that sort of thing. So they go to some shady motel, rent a room, and spend the night playing Monopoly."

"Matt hired them out to a gang lord as mercenaries. So they've been carrying out hits on previous clients, snitches, and old rivals. They probably aren't fist fights; we'd notice bruises on their knuckles. I picture Mikey as the gunman and Neil as the knifeman. But by tomorrow, the gang will view them as their own, meaning this will be our last night with them."

"Whatever they're doing, it better be good!" Art said. "We've been here for like four days without any information about what this master plan is."

"Knowing that it was Matt's idea doesn't make me feel much better," Gus confessed. "I'd almost prefer one of *our* non-serious ideas to whatever he planned." The door opened, and Mikey and Neil stepped into the room. Mikey was carrying a large, plain plastic bag.

"Hey guys!" Neil greeted. "You guys need to get ready to go."

"Go where?" Gus asked, pausing the movie he had found on Netflix.

"Just put these on and follow us." Mikey pulled black hoodies out of the bag and tossed them to each of the guys. Shrugging, Gus and Art slipped them over their heads, put their shoes on, and followed Neil out the door.

Mikey joined them in the parking lot a moment later, backpack slung over his shoulder. He motioned and started leading the group away from the motel. They zigged and zagged down side streets, seemingly avoiding the main roads as much as possible.

"Where are we going?" Gus whispered, following closely to Mikey and Neil.

"You should be able to figure it out," Neil replied. "What's directly in front of us?"

Gus recalled looking at the map of Indianapolis over the last few days. He glanced at his surroundings, but nothing stuck out as familiar or noteworthy. Ahead of them, he could see a long but low structure. As they drew closer, the structure seemed to resemble his high school football stadium, but he knew that they were not approaching the Lucas Oil Stadium.

Suddenly it hit him. "That's the Motor Speedway!" They were approaching it from the back side, so all they saw were the bleacher-like seats and the fence.

"Ding ding ding, we have a winner!" Mikey taunted. "We're going to watch some late-night Nascar!" Neil chuckled.

"Oh good, you'll bore me to death," Gus said.

"Are we breaking into the Speedway?"

"Technically, no." Neil smirked at him in the darkness. "Mikey and I already did the 'breaking in' part. Now we're just entering!"

"What's so special about this place?" Art asked, playing on his phone as they walked.

"Nothing really," Mikey said. "It's just a giant racetrack. It's been here for a long time. What's special is what we plan to do there." Gus glanced sideways to see Mikey grinning and tugging on his backpack straps.

"Mikey, what's in your backpack?"

"Don't worry about it, Gussie boy," he teased. "You'll find out soon enough."

"Boy? I'm the oldest here!" he retorted, shoving Mikey. Then he paused. "Well I might as well have fun. This will be a funny story to tell my grandchildren."

They continued walking in silence until they reached the parking lot to the Speedway. As they crossed the vast, empty space, Gus appreciated their approach from the side streets. This side of the Speedway had much less traffic at this hour, so sneaking in would be easier.

"I thought I told you to stop being a worry-wart," Neil reassured, seemingly reading Gus's mind. "We've been in this parking lot every night this week. Nobody comes back here. Well, no-body who would want any police attention any-way. Trust me!"

"Yea, I may never trust you again, especially if you're listening to Matt."

They drew near to the fence, and Gus noticed a section of broken links. He glanced at Neil, who winked without a word. Mikey led the way, pushing the two sides of the opening apart and wriggling through the gap. They found their way from under the seats out onto the track, where they paused to take in their surroundings.

Gus knew nothing about the size of the Speed-way, but it seemed to expand infinitely in every direction. No matter where he looked, he could hardly see the silhouette of the stands surround-ing the track. Simultaneously, the dark emptiness of the space seemed to crowd around him.

"Fun fact," Mikey said suddenly. "The Speed-way covers about 550 acres, which would fit around 500 football fields." His voice echoed through the vacant space around them.

"I think I would've preferred the gay bar or the hooker," Gus mused quietly.

"What are you talking about?" Neil asked.

"Oh nothing," Art answered. "Just us imagin-ing what you two were doing the last few nights.

We had some laughs."

"I don't know if there are any guards, but we should be quiet anyway," Mikey suggested. "I don't think they'd take kindly to visitors. Follow me." He led them across the middle of the track. Without any light, Gus could just make out the shapes of structures around him. They returned to the track on the opposite side of the Speedway and walked a bit further.

"Right here," Neil said, stopping. Gus looked around, confused. Then he saw that Neil was pointing to the track in front of them.

"The Yard of Bricks," Mikey explained. "A tiny remnant of the bricks that used to make up this racetrack. These mark the start and finish line." Gus saw a three-foot strip of bricks stretching the width of the track. Mikey knelt, took off his backpack, and rummaged inside it. He pulled out a wide chisel and a hammer.

"Whoa, wait," Gus interrupted, whispering. "You're not really—?" The sound of metal striking wood echoing around him, cutting him off.

"That's too much noise," Neil noted.

"Wrap your hoodie around the chisel," Gus said. Mikey nodded and obeyed. He began hammering at the bricks methodically. "It's only illegal if you get caught, right?"

"Atta boy!" Mikey cheered quietly. "We knew there was a reason we kept you around all these years."

Gus paced up and down the track and scanned the darkness intently. The dull sound of Mikey digging out the bricks continued for several minutes. As he paced, Gus watched Mikey remove first one, then two, then three bricks from the strip. He pulled a fourth from the track, wiped his forehead, and stopped.

"Alright guys," he whispered, "time for the final part." Opening his backpack again, he removed four bottles of chocolate milk and passed them around.

"You see, winners of the Indianapolis 500 always chug a glass of milk as they accept their trophy," Neil explained. "This was Mikey's personal touch. So, as we accept our trophies in the form of Speedway bricks, let us drink." Following his lead, Gus opened his bottle and downed his milk. Art fiddled with his insulin pump to account for the drink.

"Okay, we can go now." Mikey packed the empty bottles, tools, and bricks into his backpack. Pulling on his hoodie, he tossed the bag over his shoulders and jogged across the speedway.

Before long, they were safely back in the motel

room. Mikey passed out the bricks to his friends, who stuffed them in their individual suitcases.

Gus decided to take a shower before going to bed. Stepping into the shower, he stuck his head under the shower head. As the hot water trickled over his face, he thought, *What have I gotten myself into? This trip is going to be insane.*

17

Several days passed before the guys decided to leave Indianapolis. They spent most of that time in the motel room, playing cards and watching Netflix. Nothing seemed to come from their brick theft. As they packed their bags, they had to figure out their next destination.

"Mikey or Art, it's one of your turn to pick where we go," Gus began. "Maybe we can do something a little less illegal than breaking into the Motor Speedway."

"Hey, you have to admit that was fun!" Neil defended. Gus shrugged.

"Art, do you have anything you want to do in Indiana?" Mikey asked.

"Nope. I don't live here!" he replied, laughing. "You can take this one."

"Well I don't live here either. But I do have an idea. Who likes camping?" Mikey glanced up from packing to look at each of his friends. "My family has a cabin near Lake Michigan, so we can go there! We'll be able to swim, sit around a campfire, share scary stories, and whatever else we want to do!"

"Is there electricity?" Neil immediately asked.

"There's a generator out back, yea," Mikey answered. "I'll probably have to put some gas in it, but I can deal with that when we get there."

"Okay, good," Neil said, sighing. "I think I'd die if my phone died for anything longer than a few minutes. And I have no idea what we'd do if we didn't have the PlayStation." He laughed uncomfortably.

"Well they didn't have Wi-Fi when I was up there last summer," Mikey explained. "And reception is terrible, so your phone will be pretty much useless" He patted Neil on the back and took his suitcase outside.

The rest of the group followed him. Checking their snack supply, they decided to stop for gas and a bag of ice on the way north. Neil tried to call shotgun, but Gus took the seat anyway, citing his height as an excuse.

"Fine, you can take shotgun," Neil grumbled, climbing into the backseat. "But I get to pick where we eat!"

"Fine, where do you want to eat?" Mikey

asked, pulling out of the parking lot.

"Gus, you know the place," he teased. "It's a delicious little place in West Lafayette. The best root beer and the best burgers you'll ever eat."

"Triple XXX!" Gus exclaimed. "I love that place! I haven't been there in so long!"

"That sounds like a strip club or something," Art noted. "What is it?"

"Not quite. It's a family restaurant. A small drive-in restaurant in West Lafayette," Neil explained. "It's been open for like a hundred years. It brews its own root beer, which is probably the best I've ever drank."

"Okay, so can you navigate us, right?" Mikey glanced at Neil in the rearview mirror.

"Just get to West Lafayette," he replied, "then I can get you there."

"Got it." Mikey pulled out his phone, typed in their destination, and drove. "Who wants to play a game?"

"What game?" Gus asked. "Do I know this game? Better question, what reason could you give me to play this game?"

"Padiddle," Mikey said with a smirk. "Loser buys Triple XXX."

"Good enough reason for me. I'll play."

"Wait, question: how naked are we getting?"

"Let me put it this way, Neil. If anybody gets fully naked in my car, I will stop the car, pull you from your seat, beat you half to death, and leave you in a ditch." Mikey took his eyes off the road for a moment to glance at Gus and into the rearview at Neil and Art.

"So first one to lose after getting down to their boxers, got it," Neil clarified. "We'll start after the next exit."

When they exited, the boys immediately began scanning the cars around them looking for busted headlights. Whenever they saw one, screams of "Padiddle!" would fill the vehicle as they tried to be the first to shout and slap the ceiling. The last person to do so would have to remove an article of clothing.

Gus was the first to lose. "Well, time to keep my word!" He slipped off his shoes, pulled off his jeans, and put his shoes back on.

The game continued for about an hour. The four took turns removing various articles of clothing. Ultimately, as they entered West Lafayette, Neil and Gus were left in their boxers. Both scanned every passing car intently.

"Padiddle!" Gus screamed, punching the ceiling. Art and Mikey followed suit, leaving Neil as the loser.

"You guys suck," he said, laughing. They all dressed again as Neil directed Mikey toward their destination. A few minutes later, they pulled into the parking lot next to a black and orange striped building.

"Welcome to Triple XXX!" Gus exclaimed, getting out of the car. He led them up the sidewalk and into the building.

Inside, they saw a countertop weave around the room, with bar stools placed every few feet for customers. Taking their seats, they grabbed menus from the condiment caddy in front of them. As they scanned their options, a waitress approached them, walking in the space inside the countertop.

"Welcome to Triple XXX," she said apathetically, hardly looking at them. "How are you doing today?"

"Hungry!" Neil responded. "So we came to one of the best restaurants in West Lafayette! These two guys have never been here, either." He motioned at Art and Mikey.

"Well I'm sure you'll have a great time," she mumbled sarcastically. "I'm Crystal. What do you want to drink? We have Pepsi, root—"

"Root beers all around," Neil interrupted. He paused for a moment when Crystal glared at him.

"They need to try it!"

"Coming right up, Mr. Impatient." She walked off as the group continued looking over the menus. She came back a moment later with four full mugs. She pulled out her notepad to take their orders. Gus ordered the Duane Purvis, Art and Neil got the Bert, and Mikey requested the Boilermaker Pete.

"How far away is your family's cabin?" Art asked, sipping on his root beer. "Oh gosh, this is so good! I need more!"

"It's about a two-hour drive from here," Mikey answered. "We should be there by dinner time. We may even be able to fish in Lake Michigan and cook our own dinner!"

"That could be cool," Neil said. "Or we can just grab McDonald's or something."

"Or we could not," Gus replied dryly. "Art, do you have any idea where we'll go after Lake Michigan?"

"No idea. I'll look for something while we drive." Art pulled out his meter pack and checked his blood sugar. He then adjusted his pump.

"You live here in West Lafayette, don't you Neil?" Gus asked.

"Yea, born and raised. I didn't go to public school, but I know a ton of people who live, work, and go to school here. My brother would let me tag along with his friends all the time. And during my senior year of high school, my buddies and I would run around Purdue's campus with some of the college students."

"Sounds legit," Mikey replied. "I bet you could find lots to do if we were staying."

"Oh totally." Neil smirked. "I still keep in touch with plenty of the guys. In fact, I've met more and more of them through my summers at home. I could easily find us some frat parties or games of Zombies or something. Maybe we can make it back here by the end of the summer. Have some more Triple XXX, meet some new people, have some fun."

Crystal returned with their food, passing out baskets of burgers and fries to each of the guys. She refilled their mugs and turned to walk away.

"Hey Crystal," Gus called. "Care to chat a bit? We'll share our fries if you want."

"What a charmer," she retorted. "Why do you want to talk to me? In case you haven't noticed, I'm not exactly a people person."

"Do you go to Purdue?" Neil asked suddenly. "You look a little familiar, like I may have seen you on campus sometime."

"Yea, I do." She stopped talking, then sighed

exasperatedly when the boys looked at her expectantly. "Veterinary science, with a minor in business. I'm currently taking the seven-year program, but who knows if I'll actually graduate."

"Sounds like a couple of guys I know," Mikey mumbled, nudging Gus gently. The two laughed as Art elbowed Gus and Neil punched Mikey.

"That's an interesting combination," Art noted through a mouthful of fries. "What do you want to do with your degree?"

"What every vet science major wants: to become a stripper." She chuckled lightly at her response. "I'm from Marion, which is about an hour and a half east of here. There aren't any nearby vets, so I want to open a clinic there. Wait, why am I telling you this?"

"Well we did ask," Gus replied. "I guess you're more of a people person than you think!"

"Yea, no," she said, deadpanning. "So what about you bozos? What do you study?"

"I got this," Mikey answered. "We're from Central Illinois U. Gus and I graduated a few weeks ago with degrees in philosophy and elementary education. Art and Neil over there want to be a counselor and a musician, but you'll probably open your clinic before they graduate."

"You're quite the interesting group," Crystal

noted. "Probably the most interesting guys I've met here in a long time."

"Oh really?" Neil asked. "What kind of guys do you normally meet?"

"Just the usual college sleazebags," she said, rolling her eyes. "All they do is hoot and holler and cat-call at me. They're usually horny and drunk frat boys. But then I tell them that I'm a lesbian and they...react very differently than you." The boys exchanged looks and shrugged.

"I'm guessing they lose interest pretty quickly," Gus said.

"Or it shuts them up for a bit," Mikey added.

"Yea, if only," she agreed. "There are a few who stop, but most seem to try *harder* when they hear that. Hoping for a threesome, I'm sure."

"Yea, we don't care," Art explained. "We came here to eat and take a quick break on our way to Lake Michigan, not to hook up with the waitress."

"Wait, that's not what we're doing?" Neil joked, looking around confused.

"Well you aren't hooking up with me, Mr. Impatient," Crystal replied, smirking. "Do you guys want anything else?"

"Nah, we'll take our checks and let you get back to shooting down all men who walk in here," Gus said. "Actually, Mr. Impatient is paying, so *he'll* take the check."

"Here you go. Thanks for not being douches like every other guy ever. Now get the hell out of here, especially you, Mr. Impatient."

Gus dropped some cash for a tip as they waved goodbye. Neil stopped to pay at the register while the rest of them got into Mikey's SUV. When Neil joined them, Mikey pulled out of the lot and headed north.

18

A couple of hours passed, full of loud music, road trip games, and storytelling. Mikey began weaving through side roads looking for the cabin. Gus stared out the window, watching the scenery fly past them as Neil and Art talked *League of Legends* in the back.

"Here it is!" Mikey yelled suddenly. Gus looked and saw a small cabin hidden amidst the trees. It was exactly what he expected: a small, brown building surrounded by trees.

"Where's the lake?" he asked, glancing around eagerly.

"There's a trail out back that takes you right to it," Mikey replied. "It's about a half-mile walk, though." He turned the vehicle around and backed up right to the door.

The door opened to a large room. A large flat-screen TV hung on the wall, with a pair of leather couches angled toward it. A small kitchenette sat in the far corner, with some cabinets, a fridge, and a microwave. Two doors stood along the left wall; the first led to a small bedroom with a queen-sized bed, and the other led to the bathroom.

Gus, Art, and Neil unloaded their belongings, scattering around the living room of the cabin. As they explored, Mikey went around back to check on the generator. Gus and Art loaded their food and drinks into the fridge, while Neil plopped down on the couch.

"We should be good on gas for about a week," Mikey said, walking into the cabin. "The generator is full, and there are a couple of gas cans in the shed. Also, dibs on the bedroom."

"Dibs on sharing the bedroom!" Gus shouted, shutting the fridge door. He and Mikey took their suitcases into the other room and lined some pillows along the middle of the bed as a boundary.

"So what are we doing?" Neil asked as they returned to the living room.

"Well, we can go down to the lake and swim, have a campfire, stargaze, or play games," Mikey explained. "Take your pick."

"I say we chill tonight," he replied. "Eat some junk food, play some video games, and sleep well. Then we can party hard the next few days!"

Nodding, Mikey unpacked the PlayStation

and started up a game of Spelunky. Art brought four cans of Dr. Pepper from the fridge and handed them out. The guys sat down and grabbed controllers to play. The next several hours were full of yelling, laughing, and snacking on chips and Lunchables.

Around one o'clock, the guys shut down their game. They found a movie on a shelf by the television and started playing it. The guys kicked up the leg rests on the couch and reclined. Within an hour, they were all fast asleep.

The next afternoon, the four dressed and walked down to the lake. They brought a backpack full of snacks and drinks so that they could stay for a while. Mikey had a Frisbee in his trunk, so he carried that along, passing it back and forth between his friends.

When they stepped onto the beach, they paused to take in the scenery. Sand stretched before them for about fifty yards before stopping at the water. The lake continued beyond the horizon, so they could not see the other shore. To either side of them, the beach was the only thing visible. Gus could see what looked like a city on the horizon, slightly to the left of them. He figured that it was likely Chicago.

The group set down their towels and backpack, then took off their shirts and shoes. Mikey hurled the Frisbee down the beach. Gus darted after it, dodging the other beachgoers. The Frisbee began its descent toward the water, and Gus dove, grabbed it, and splashed into the water.

Surfacing, he saw Neil jog towards him and tossed the disc to him. Thus began a game of Frisbee that spread across the immediate area. Random strangers joined them as it progressed. They never exchanged names, just shouts of "I'm open!" and "Over here!" After a group of about a dozen joined them, they formed two teams and started playing Ultimate Frisbee. The game began as two-hand touch but quickly progressed into full-tackle. As it continued, some people left, new people joined, and teams were shuffled. From time to time, they took a brief break to cool off in the water, grab something to eat and drink, and reapply sunscreen.

Around sunset, the strangers departed to go their separate ways. Mikey tucked the Frisbee into his backpack and sat down in the sand, close enough to the water for the waves to splash over his feet. Gus took a seat next to him, while Art and

Neil retrieved the last of the snacks before joining them. They sat in silence, staring across the ocean as the sun set.

"This sure is a sight," Neil muttered. "I don't think I've seen a sunset like this ever in my life." The sky was painted in layers of blue, purple, and pink. The colors continually shifted and changed as the sun sank further behind the horizon.

"I've been here dozens of times," Mikey replied. "But no two sunsets are ever the same. I try not to come up here often because I don't want to take it for granted. This is such a good place to sit and think about life." The group fell silent for a moment, listening to the crashing waves and the rustling leaves.

"So what are you thinking about?" Gus asked, eyes glued to the horizon.

"Life. The future, mostly." Mikey sighed and started dragging his finger through the sand absentmindedly. "I can't stop thinking about how ill-prepared I am for real adulthood. Dad never taught me anything. I've had to learn for myself how to write a resume, conduct myself in a job interview, pay bills, and manage my money. Now I get to have more responsibility with absolutely no idea of how to handle it. Just thinking about it is overwhelming. Yea, I'm sure it'll be great and fine, but I'm always wondering if I'm doing things right. Y'know?"

"I feel you man," Gus said. "None of us have picture-perfect dads. We're all royally screwed. Nobody taught us how to make friends, talk to girls, figure out who we are, or anything. Life without a dad sucks. I wouldn't wish this on anybody, not even Brock."

"It's almost like," Neil began, pausing briefly, "Like someone drove us out into the middle of the lake, tossed us into the water, and left. No direction, no life jacket, no instructions on how to swim. Just us and cold, suffocating water as far as the eye can see. Then we spent the rest of our lives struggling against the waves and the current to get to shore so we can finally rest and breathe. It was sink or swim, and it took everything just to keep our heads above water."

"It's not fair," Art added. "I know Mikey and I have our dads still, but that doesn't make it much better. They weren't the dads we wanted or needed; they were the dads they knew to be. Which sucked. Do you know how hard it is to have this bar set above your head that you'll never, ever reach? That you don't even want to reach? The pressure is unbearable at times! So I don't think about it. I push it out of my mind, try to lower the bar. But nobody understands."

"Nobody understands?" Neil repeated. "You don't even know. My dad's *dead*. Mikey, Art, at least your dads are around. They may suck, but you can talk to them, you can work things out. It can get better! And Gus, I get it, your dad's never been around. But maybe he'll change his mind! He's still alive, so there's a chance that you can reach out to him, talk to him, and maybe, just maybe, have a relationship. But me? I go to a slab of marble with his name on it, sitting above the casket where he's buried, and nothing. I can talk all I want, but he'll never respond. He's gone, and he's never coming back."

"That's true," Gus agreed solemnly. "But your dad didn't choose to leave. Not that it was easy or nice, but he was involved in your life until he literally could not be. But Brock, he never chose me. He always picked something else: his job, his money, his sex life, his wife or whatever, his other kid. Now I get to live with this gnawing feeling inside that I was never good enough for him. I may never be able to understand your situation fully, but none of you can truly empathize with me. Mine has been a life of fighting the man who was never there. And that invisible man wins, far more than I'd like to admit."

"You know, I like the illustration you gave a second ago," Mikey said. "Sink or swim. Isn't that true of countless other circumstances in life? Ideally, moms and dads, brothers and sisters, friends and teachers all work together to teach you how to stay afloat and to find direction. But inevitably stuff happens. Parents leave, siblings fight, and everyone else seems clueless about what to do. Then you either teach yourself to swim, or you sink and drown."

"Back on the subject of fathers, think about how that affects people our age," Art continued. "So many of them spend all of their time and effort chasing him down. They follow him everywhere he goes and do everything he does. But they don't notice that they're sinking, drowning. Instead of looking for the stability of shore, they chase after the boat that tossed them to the waves in the first place. They swim in the wrong direction and end up drowning."

"And to make matters worse, there's Father's Day." Neil began scooping up handfuls of sand and letting it sift through his fingers. "Every year, we get a stupid reminder that we're barely keeping our heads above water. That our lives suck compared to others'. And if that wasn't enough, we have social media now. We get to see dozens and dozens of posts from our friends and peers about how great their dads are."

"And each one of those posts can wash us a little farther from shore, pull us a little deeper beneath the waves we're struggling to escape," Mikey finished.

The sun had disappeared below the horizon, leaving the sky a dark, star-speckled expanse. With the colors of sunset gone, the somber mood lingered around the boys and seeped into their hearts. After a few moments, Neil stood up and wandered from the group. His friends watched as rocks flew over their heads and splashed into the water. Soon the four scoured the beach for rocks to hurl into the lake.

With every rock, they grunted and yelled to vent their frustration. The grunts and yells quickly transformed into words.

"Why'd you have to die?"

"Thanks for nothing!"

"Stop living through me!"

"Let me live my life!"

"It's not fair!"

"Why am I never good enough?"

"I hate you!"

"I don't want to be a doctor!"

"I wasn't ready to grow up!"

"Sometimes I wish you were dead!"

"I don't need you!"

"Where were you when *I* needed my dad?"

"I can't handle all of this pressure!"

"Look at me now! I did it!"

"Why do I still miss you?"

"Do you realize how much you hurt me?"

"I'm so scared to be like you!"

"It's not fair!"

"Why did you do this to me?"

"I hope you're happy now!"

"I never needed you anyway!"

"Are you proud of me now?"

The yelling slowly reverted to incoherent shouts and grunts. As the rocks became sparse, the shouts faded into silence as the four boys stood on the beach. They stared at the lake wordlessly, panting.

"It's not fair," Mikey growled finally. "It's not fair that our dads suck. It's not fair that we have to struggle through every moment of life because of something that we couldn't control! It's not fair that we have to figure out everything on our own and live with this pain, this weight every second of our lives. It's not fair that nobody understands how we feel, and it's not fair that there's nothing they can do to help us. None of it is fair!

"But here we are. Against all odds, we made it. We swam. Through all the weight, all the pain, all the unfairness, we made it to shore. We learned to swim, we kept our heads above the waves, and we never gave up. Now we're on the shore, looking at what lies behind us, what lies before us. After swimming for so long, we don't know how to walk on the land. But we'll figure it out. We've made it this far; we have no choice but to keep going. So we will."

The group fell silent. The wind continued to blow around them. The waves crashed against the shore, dampening their feet.

"Amen," Neil whispered. "Amen."

19

After that night, the guys stayed at the cabin for a few more days. They spent another day or two on the beach, swimming and playing Frisbee with other beachgoers. When they were not at the beach, they watched movies, played Spelunky, and ate junk food. One night, Mikey and Art drove to the nearest town for food, while Gus and Neil searched the nearby woods for firewood.

"What exactly are we looking for?" Neil asked, kicking absentmindedly at the ground.

"Dude, have you never had a campfire?"

"I lived in the city! I've never made a fire!"

"Fair enough. Pick up a ton of small and medium sized sticks and a bunch of leaves. And make sure they're dry. We need kindling to start the fire. I'll chop some of these small trees into firewood." Neil wandered the woods, while Gus headed to the shed to look for an ax. Finding one, he hacked away at some nearby saplings, cutting them down and then splitting them into logs.

By the time Mikey and Art returned, they had made distinct piles of leaves, twigs, and logs by the cabin. Mikey and Gus built a fire pit behind the cabin, digging a shallow hole and surrounding it with rocks from the beach. As they made a fire, Neil and Art grabbed some lawn chairs from the shed and set them around the pit. The fire roared to life before them.

"This is the life," Mikey sighed, taking a seat.

"So when's dinner?" Art asked. "We bought all sorts of food, but when are we making it?"

"Whenever you want," Mikey replied. "The sticks are in the shed, and we have hotdogs and supplies for s'mores in the cabin." Gus went to the shed and brought back four sticks as Neil retrieved the food.

The next few hours passed as the guys relaxed by the fire. Neil and Art never seemed to stop eating, always having their sticks in the fire to cook hotdogs or roast marshmallows. Mikey and Gus shared various stories of camping from high school. After a while, the conversation moved to the next leg of their trip.

"So Art," Neil began through a huge bite of hotdog, "where are we going next?"

"Umm," he stammered. "We could totally go

to Chicago."

"What would we do there?" Neil asked.

"We could visit the Bean," Art suggested. "I don't think Gus has ever been to Chicago, so it would be kind of cool."

"Question," Gus interrupted. "Did you even think of anything? Or did you just come up with that on the spot?"

"Um yes," he replied, laughing.

"Oh Art," Neil muttered, shaking his head. "I don't know why we expected anything else from you. You do everything at the last minute."

"Chicago could be fun!" Art pulled out his phone and started typing on it. "I can look up plenty of things to do!"

"Well, it's his decision!" Neil declared. "We're going to Chicago!" Gus and Mikey glanced at each other and shrugged. They began discussing the various attractions in Chicago that they could visit. Art remained determined to visit the Bean.

"Here's a fun idea," Art said. "The Skydeck."

"Wait, is that what I think it is?" Gus asked.

"It's the observation deck on Willis Tower," Mikey explained. "You basically stand outside the tower on a pane of glass."

"Yea, nope," Gus interrupted. "Not a fan of heights. I'd rather die, thank you very much."

"Live a little, bro," Neil taunted. "You won't die! Tons of people visit it each year without plummeting to their deaths."

Gus sighed and shook his head. "I'm going to regret this, but fine. Let's go to the Skydeck. It sounds like a big tourist attraction. But I have one condition: we have to take all of the stereotypical tourist photos."

"Oh yes!" Art shouted excitedly. "We'll be the best tourists."

They continued laughing and joking as the sun set. Snacks ran out shortly after sunset, but they stayed around the fire until it dwindled. By midnight, it was a pile of smoldering logs.

"Let's head inside," Mikey said. Neil and Art went straight inside and showered. Mikey put the chairs and sticks back in the shed, while Gus spread the ashes and poured a bucket of lake water over them.

A couple of hours later, the guys had claimed their beds: Mikey and Gus in the bed, and Art and Neil on the couches. They passed out almost instantly and slept until nearly noon. After waking up, they ate a quick breakfast of deli sandwiches and loaded the car. They stopped at the first laundromat they found to wash laundry before heading to Chicago.

Once in the city, they headed for Willis Tower. Mikey pointed it out to Gus as they drew closer, and his stomach dropped. It was the tallest building in the city, and he could see several protruding boxes of glass way above them.

Gus began dreading the Skydeck as they parked and entered the building. They stepped into the elevator, and the doors closed. As it rose to the floors above, Gus winced and swayed on his feet as his ears popped from the changing air pressure. The display above the panel read "103" when the elevator stopped and the doors opened.

Mikey led the group to the glass boxes, which were full of people. As they waited, the building around them swayed slightly, tightening Gus's stomach into knots. To distract himself, he pulled out his phone and researched the tower.

"Apparently, the boxes are affectionately called 'the Ledge,'" he read. "They stand 1,353 feet above the pavement. Which, on a side note, is only 150 feet too short to reach terminal velocity. Each box retracts back into the building so that they can be cleaned easily. Oh gosh, one of the panes of glass shattered in 2014 while tourists were in the box. That makes me feel so much better. Willis Tower is also the tallest building in America. The World Trade Center surpassed it for a while, until 9/11. On a clear day, tourists can see—oof!" Gus was cut off by a shove from behind. One of the Ledges had emptied, and Neil directed him toward it. He stumbled onto the glass and glanced downwards.

"Oh gosh," he murmured. Immediately lightheaded, he doubled over, planted his hands against the glass wall, and closed his eyes. He breathed slowly as his friends joined him.

"What do you think, Gus?" Neil taunted, patting him on the back.

"Shut up," he replied through gritted teeth.

"If you'd stop looking down, it's actually a really good view." Mikey's voice came from behind him. Inhaling, he straightened himself shakily and opened his eyes.

Around him, the city of Chicago spanned for what seemed like miles. In the distance, Gus could see Lake Michigan stretching from the city to the horizon. Looking to the right, he saw Chicago give way to open fields. Though Gus hated heights, the view around him made him forget all about his uneasiness.

"Could you imagine being up here for sunrise or sunset?" Mikey asked. "The view would be even more beautiful."

"What about during a thunderstorm?" Neil

added. "Seeing the rain and lightning from such a high vantage point would be cool. And seeing a funnel cloud form would be so unreal."

"I wonder how busy this place is for the Fourth," Gus mused. "I know there are huge fireworks shows around Lake Michigan. That would be another sight to behold."

"Shut up and enjoy the view that we do have," Art mumbled.

"Oh snap, Art's being serious!" Gus replied, laughing. "You know, I'm glad it wasn't Neil's idea to come here. He'd probably have us rappelling down from the SkyDeck in the middle of the night. I obviously would have had to kill him before that happened."

The group fell silent. After a few moments, Gus left the box and waited in the hallway. His friends joined him shortly afterward. Without a word, they returned to the elevator and descended to the ground floor.

"Oh sweet terra firma!" Gus exclaimed once they stepped outside. He excitedly jumped around, stomping his feet.

"You never answered my question," Neil said. "How was it?"

"Worst thirty seconds or whatever of my life," Gus replied. "The view was nice, but like I said,

I'd rather die than go back up there. I prefer keeping my feet on solid ground."

"So where's the Bean?" Art asked. Mikey glanced around to get his bearings before pointing directly in front of them.

"We could probably walk," he added. "It's not too far. A handful of blocks."

The guys started walking, weaving through the crowded Chicago streets. Gus spent much of the walk taking in his surroundings. Mikey shared information about the various shops and sights in the city, having grown up near the city. After a while, they entered Millennium Park.

Directly ahead of them sat something resembling a giant reflective jelly bean. It towered above the tourists crowding around it. Through the crowds, Gus noticed people walking under the bean, as there was an arch to provide space. Many of the people in the park were taking photos of the giant sculpture.

"Interesting," Gus said. "I've seen plenty of pictures on Facebook, so it's not impressive. But it's interesting to see how much attention it gets."

"Yea, it's a huge tourist attraction," Mikey explained. "We need to get a picture with it. No complaints, Gus! When in Chicago, do as the Chicagoans do!"

"I have an idea," Neil added. "Let's get everyone here involved in a huge group photo!"

Without waiting for a response, he and Art hurried toward the crowd and started speaking loudly to the strangers. Mikey and Neil followed as everyone lined up in front of the Bean. Neil handed his phone to a random person, who backed away from the structure.

"Okay, we'll stand here," Neil directed. Gus and Mikey moved to where he pointed, and Neil and Art joined them. Suddenly the people behind them lifted them off the ground.

"Whoa whoa, what the heck?" Mikey exclaimed. Art and Neil started laughing.

"I forgot to mention that I convinced them to toss us into the air for the picture," Neil replied. "Here's hoping they don't drop us!"

"Neil, when we're done here, we're going to kill you!" Gus yelled.

"Are you guys ready?" the stranger with Neil's phone asked. "3...2...1...go!" He touched the screen to start taking pictures as the crowd heaved and threw the four guys into the air. They cried out in surprise as they rose and then fell back to the strangers below them. A couple of men managed to catch each of the guys and put them on their feet.

"Thanks guys! I'll find a good picture and tweet it, so make sure you all follow me on Twitter!" Neil shouted to the crowd. He retrieved his phone and started walking back toward the car, his friends at his heels.

"How did you convince them to toss us like cheerleaders?" Mikey asked.

"I told them it was Gus's bachelor party, so we wanted to make sure he had an extra special picture at the Bean," Neil replied, grinning.

"You're stupid," Gus retorted. "It's obviously Mikey's bachelor party. Anyway, where are we going now?"

"I think we'll just crash at a hotel," Mikey said. "Then we can figure out what we'll do next. Maybe we'll agree on something to do, or we can just go through us all again."

"Sounds like a plan. We should consider getting something substantial to eat," Art added. "All the junk and Lunchables are getting old."

"So what's good in Chicago?" Neil asked, turning to Mikey.

"What else besides pizza?" he answered. "There's a good place not too far from here called Lou's. We can call in some carry-out, pick it up, and find a hotel."

"I do enjoy pizza," Art agreed. "Let's do that."

Mikey pulled out his phone and dialed a number. He ordered a large pepperoni deep-dish pizza with extra cheese. Hanging up the phone, the group continued their trek back to their parking lot. Returning to their vehicle, they drove to Lou's and picked up their pizza. Afterward, Mikey found a nearby hotel, and they settled into their room for the night.

"This pizza is so good!" Neil exclaimed, a long string of cheese dripping from his full mouth.

"I know, right?" Mikey agreed. "Chicago is literally famous for deep-dish pizza! Everyone should try it at least once in their lives." The conversation died as the four of them devoured the pizza. They then turned on the television and found a random channel to watch while taking turns in the shower.

"Isn't Father's Day soon?" Art asked after all showers were done.

"Um it's this weekend," Gus answered. "We should do something special for it. And by special, I mean something fun that distracts us from social media and everything."

"We should go to D'Arcy's," Neil suggested. "It's impossible to be sad when we're stuffing our faces with horseshoes!"

"Good point," Mikey agreed. "We'll do that

this weekend. What shall we do until then?"

"Eh, we'll figure it out later," Art said. He pulled out his Vita and tuned out the conversation around him.

"What's there to do in Chicago?" Gus started searching for things to do with his phone.

"We don't even need to leave the hotel," Neil said after a moment. Gus looked up to see him holding a brochure for their hotel. "They have a pool and a hot tub."

"All right, I'm sold." Mikey clapped his hands together excitedly. "Let's enjoy a week of relaxation and refreshment."

20

Gus woke up first, around noon the next day. He decided to find the hot tub, so he put on a pair of shorts and a t-shirt and grabbed a towel. Writing a quick note to tell the guys where he was, he left the room and started wandering the hotel.

He found the hot tub in an isolated room next to the pool. It was empty, so he went in, took off his shirt, and lowered himself into the warm water. He reclined so that the water covered his shoulders and rested his head on the floor outside the hot tub, closing his eyes. Gus was starting to doze off when the door into the room opened.

"Hey man," Mikey greeted. "I saw your note and figured you'd enjoy some company. And some music!" He gestured towards a sound system in the corner. He hooked up his phone and slid into the hot tub across from Gus. Soft instrumental music filled the room.

"This sounds like the film scores station on

Pandora," Gus noted.

"That's because it is," Mikey replied, chuckling. "It's very relaxing, non-distracting music. Plus, it's all beautifully composed."

"Any idea when Art and Neil will get up?"

"Knowing them, about dinner time. Though I did text them before starting the music to wake them up. Maybe they'll be here soon."

At that moment, the door opened, and the two entered the room. For some reason, they were laughing hysterically. Neil climbed into the hot tub with the guys, while Art sat on the edge with his feet in the water, drinking Mountain Dew.

"What's up?" Art asked.

"Well I just woke up and decided to soak in the hot tub," Gus answered. "It's very relaxing. I've never been in a hot tub before. How's your blood sugar?"

"A little low, as normal. Hence the Dew."

"You've never been in a hot tub? They're so great!" Neil interrupted, sinking lower into the water so that it covered his chin.

"It is really nice. I'm probably going to relax here for a while."

"We should go back and grab some snacks sometime," Neil added. "But otherwise, I'm right here with you!"

The boys fell silent, listening to the music and the bubbling of the hot tub. Gus finally broke the silence. "You know what's dumb? Father's Day. Father's Day is dumb."

"I hear you," Art agreed. "It's not even fun for me, and my dad's around."

"Seriously," Neil added. "We don't need a reminder of how much our lives suck. I don't know about you guys, but my mind takes care of that quite well. I mean, I do have some fun memories of Dad, but mostly it's just a depressing day."

"Yea, my dad usually makes it all about him." Mikey shook his head. "He tries to act like he's the best person in the world, but he's not perfect by any means."

"It also doesn't help that Brock's birthday is next weekend," Gus said. "So it's always a double-whammy. This is just a long week of thinking about Brock and why he isn't around."

"Definitely not a fun time," Neil agreed.

"We'll have to keep your mind off all that next week," Mikey suggested. "We can find a bunch of really fun things to do, like DBZ Abridged. All else fails, I'll drive us to the East Coast or to New York or something. Take you somewhere new and exciting, get you out of the Midwest."

Gus forced a laugh. "Sounds like a plan. I

don't think we'll need to go that far, but we can keep that as an option. The least we should do is stay off our phones. That way, we won't have to see all of the 'my dad is so awesome' posts."

"Hopefully Father's Day will be more enjoyable when we get married and become dads ourselves," Art said. "Then we can focus on loving our wives and kids instead of on the father-shaped holes in our lives. On a different note, what else is there to do in the Midwest? Maybe we check out some new places and sights."

"There's St. Louis," Mikey said. "There's the Gateway Arch and the zoo."

"There's Turkey Run State Park back in Indiana," Neil added. "It has some really great hiking trails, horseback riding, and camping."

"We could always go to Tennessee!" Gus chimed in. "There's plenty to do in Knoxville, and then Nashville is the heart of country music."

"No." Neil's face deadpanned. "You know I hate country music." Gus laughed and punched him in the arm.

"See!" Mikey exclaimed. "There are options. We'll find something to do next week. It'll be a good time!"

They continued sharing ideas of things to visit around the Midwest. Art recorded their ideas on his phone, as he remained out of the water due to his insulin pump. When they ran out of their own ideas, Art searched for new locations and sights with his phone. After a while, they had an expansive list of options.

"Well, my skin is getting all clammy," Neil said suddenly. "Let's go back to the room and grab some food. Maybe go out for dinner after we watch a movie."

"Dibs on the pizza Lunchables!" Gus quickly climbing out of the hot tub. He picked up his towel and shirt and darted out of the room. He made it to the room first, found the keycard folded in his towel, and opened the door.

The guys turned on the PlayStation after changing clothes. After starting *Parks and Recreation* again, they grabbed Lunchables and cans of Dr. Pepper from the fridge and sat down on the beds. Neil also found an unopened bag of chips and started passing it around.

"So what sounds good for dinner?" Mikey asked. "American? Chinese? Italian?"

"Chinese," Art said immediately. "Is that even a question?"

"I agree. We've had tons of American food. Maybe we'll have Italian some other time," Gus added. Neil shrugged indifferently.

"Okay, so let's see what we have around here." Mikey pulled out his phone and started typing away at the screen. "There's an Asian grill and sushi bar! Who likes sushi?"

"Go there!" Gus exclaimed. "I love sushi! And it's a grill for you guys to eat something that isn't as good as sushi."

"Any objections?" Mikey glanced at Art and Neil, and both shook their heads. "All right, to the bar and grill! After a few more episodes of *Parks and Rec*."

21

A few hours later, they sat down around a large griddle. After ordering their drinks, they looked through the menus. Gus was intent on getting sushi, while Art and Neil wanted sweet and spicy chicken. Mikey weighed his options and decided to get grilled shrimp and steak. The waiter, a quiet young man named Phillip, returned to pass out their drinks and record their orders before disappearing back into the kitchen.

"I'm so excited for this," Neil said. "I love watching the chefs prepare our food."

"Your food," Gus sassed. "You don't cook sushi, dummy."

"Well see if we share anything with you!" Neil threw his crumpled up straw wrapper across the counter at Gus.

"I'm definitely not sharing mine," Mikey said. "I got the surf and turf!"

"Fine, no sushi for any of you guys either!"

His friends started retching and gagging.

After a few minutes, their chef approached the table. He pushed a cart covered in various bottles and ingredients, including vegetables, rice, and meat. He sprayed some oil on the griddle and picked up a turner and meat fork.

"Hello, my name is Vincent. How are you guys today?" he asked, firing up the grill. He started his routine with his utensils, clattering and flipping them across the griddle.

"We're good!" Mikey replied, grinning broadly. "We're ready for some authentic Asian food, so it's going to be a good night! I'm Mikey, and these are Neil, Art, and Gus. How are you?"

"Nice to meet you. I'm good," he replied. He sprayed more oil and lit it. "Watch your eyebrows." He poured more oil across the griddle and flames sprang to life, climbing toward the ceiling. Heat seared the boys' faces.

"Whoa!" Neil yelled. "This is definitely my favorite part of Asian grills."

"Keep watching," Vincent said. "It's going to be good." He oiled the griddle again before dumping a large bowl of rice onto it. As he mixed it and added oil, he continued flipping his utensils around each other and his hands.

"How long does it take to learn all these

tricks?" Gus asked, amazed. All four of them had their eyes glued to the griddle, watching the man's show.

"Many, many hours. I trained for many years at a secret chef school in the Chinese mountains, learning all the recipes and tricks by heart." Vincent laughed heartily at his own joke, making his customers laugh as well. He dumped a plate of vegetables on another part of the griddle, oiling and mixing them so that they could cook. "But really, I grew up in a restaurant in China. My parents taught me everything I know. So now I work hard to provide for my family."

"That's cool!" Gus exclaimed. "How many kids do you have?"

"I have three. The oldest is thirteen, and the youngest is six," he explained. "My wife left after the youngest was born, so I've been raising them alone for six years."

"Dang, that's a bummer," Neil said quietly.

"Yes, it is hard. But I work hard every day to provide for them. I make sure I'm home to cook dinner and help with their homework. There is nothing that I wouldn't do for them. Those kids are my world. Family comes first, always."

"That's true," Gus said.

"Unfortunately that's not always the case,"

Mikey added. "Too many parents leave their kids nowadays. People like you, Vincent, are the exception."

Vincent grabbed a couple of shakers and covered the cooking food in spices. "That is true. It explains why so many people your age are broken and hurting. If dads would do their jobs, half of the problems in the world would be gone."

"Well no worries!" Mikey replied. "We're going to be the best dads in the world one day, so we'll change the world!" He grinned broadly and laughed.

"Good! Keep that attitude!" he replied. Vincent looked up at the guys. "Which of you got shrimp and steak? And you two got sweet and spicy chicken?" Mikey raised his hand for the first question, and Art and Neil nodded in response to the second.

"And I got the sushi!" Gus interrupted. "I don't want you forgetting that."

"Oh I won't." The chef turned to Art and Neil. "How do you want your chicken? More sweet, more spicy, little of both?" He dumped a plate of diced chicken onto the grill, along with a small plate of diced steak and shrimp.

"We like it a little spicy," Neil said.

"That's something we have in common, my

friend!" The man laughed and grabbed a bottle of orange sauce, dousing the chicken in it. "I have a little seasoning here that I think you'll like, Mr. Surf and Turf." He covered the steak and shrimp in a light brown sauce.

"I'll take your word for it!" Mikey agreed. "Judging from your cooking skills, you know what you're talking about!"

"And now you're Mr. Brown-Nose," Vincent teased, chuckling. "Here, take some rice!" He divided the rice among three plates. He followed this with the vegetables after cutting and mixing them. A small pile of rice and vegetables remained, so he pulled an empty plate from his cart and moved the piles to it.

"All right, I see everyone else's food, but where's my sushi?"

"Oh, did you not read the fine print?" The man glanced at Gus and smirked. "You have to go to the lake and catch your own fish!" He covered both piles of meat in more sauce and continued to mix them.

"I guess I'll just have to snag some food from these guys!" Gus picked up his fork, leaned across the counter, and stole a piece of broccoli from Art.

"Sneaky dude!" With a laugh, Vincent divided the chicken among Art and Neil's plates, after which he added an extra spray of sauce. He then transferred the steak and shrimp to Mikey's plate. He deliberately left several pieces of each and added them to the fourth plate.

"Thanks so much!" Art declared. He stuffed his Vita back into his pocket and pulled his plate toward him.

"Welcome back to reality, my brother!"

Neil nudged Art's arm and whispered, "It's funny because you're Chinese."

"I'm half!" Art yelled, flailing his arms at Neil. "I'm only half! Thanks Dad."

"Before I go, I have one last thing to give." The chef reached into his cart and pulled out a plate with two sushi rolls on it. "Your lame sushi. And because I feel bad for you, here's a little sampler platter of what your friends are eating! Thanks for the conversation, guys, and best wishes in changing the world." He handed both plates to Gus and walked away with his cart.

"That guy was awesome," Neil said. "He had such a good sense of humor."

"Definitely," Mikey agreed. "We need to tip extra well. But in the meantime, it's time to dig in!" Without another word, he picked up his fork and started eating.

"This was probably the best decision we've made in Chicago," Art commented, his mouth was full of rice and chicken.

"Would it kill you to swallow your food before you speak?" Gus asked. "It's actually quite gross when you do that." In response, both Neil and Art opened their mouths and stuck out their tongues, showing Gus their half-chewed food.

"One of the best things about Chinese places," Neil began, "is that they always give you so much food! There's always enough to fill you up and still take a full meal home!"

"Gus, if you take any of that sushi home, you're walking back to the hotel." Mikey locked eyes with him and stared. Unfazed, Gus lifted a piece of sushi to his mouth and bit into it. Slowly he tore his bite away, turning his head away from Mikey and closing his eyes. He added a soft grunt for extra effect.

Neil blinked a few times, confused. "Did you just…eat a piece of sushi seductively?"

"As a matter of fact, I did," Gus replied, smirking. "Are you seduced?"

"That's it, I'm done!" Mikey exclaimed, throwing his hands into the air. "Waiter, we're ready for our checks!"

Gus laughed and accepted a high five from Art. Shaking his head, Mikey downed the rest of his drink and tried not to smile. Phillip walked over to the table a moment later and passed out their checks.

"How was everything?" he mumbled quickly.

"It was delicious!" Neil answered as they each dug their wallets from their back pockets.

"I agree!" Gus added. "The food was amazing, and we really enjoyed our chef."

"Good," he replied. "Would you guys like take-home boxes?"

"Yes please!" Mikey agreed. They handed their receipts back to him with their debit cards, and he nodded and left.

"What should we do now?" Gus asked, popping his last piece of sushi into his mouth.

"No idea," Mikey said.

"We'll figure it out. We don't need to figure it out yet." Neil laughed when he saw Gus rolling his eyes. "Just go with the flow, bro. Planning ahead is lame."

"Well so far, 'the flow' has been 'watching Netflix for hours on end,'" Gus retorted. "And planning ahead is what kept me from having to pull all-nighters to finish papers when I was a college student."

"'When I was a college student,'" Neil repeated mockingly. "You just graduated. Also, at least I get the papers done! Eventually." He shrugged and laughed awkwardly.

Phillip returned to the table carrying four Styrofoam boxes. He handed one to each of the guys, then pulled their debit cards and receipts from his apron pocket and passed them out. After setting a few pens on the counter, he wished them a good night and walked away quickly.

"All right, let's roll," Mikey said. They scraped their leftovers into their boxes, signed their receipts, and headed back to the hotel.

22

"I'm going for a walk. I need some fresh air. You're welcome to join me, but I'm leaving now." Gus stood up, stretched, and grabbed his wallet.

"Sweet! Where are we going?" Mikey jumped up and turned off the PlayStation. "We'll join you. I think we all could benefit from fresh air and stretching our legs."

"I'm not sure," Gus replied. "I'm going to start walking and go into the first place that seems interesting."

"This could be a lot of fun!" Neil slipped on his shoes and stepped into the hallway.

Gus led the group out of the hotel. Out on the sidewalk, he paused for a moment before turning and walking down a random street. They walked for several blocks, glancing into the windows of every business they passed.

"What sounds interesting?" Art asked. "We have coffee shops, fast food, souvenir shops, clothing stores, banks, and a couple of candy stores." Neil and Mikey joined him in reading the signs hanging above them.

"Well I don't drink coffee, so that's out of the question," Gus answered. "And I'm not looking for a bank that's like four hours from home."

"Jeez Gus, you're so hard to please!" Neil joked. "If you don't make a decision, I'll have to choose something!"

"Bro, there's nothing wrong with a leisurely stroll through downtown," Mikey retorted. "If we don't find anything to do, we can just go back to the hotel and get back to the normal routine."

"We should at least grab something to drink," Art added. "My blood sugar feels a little low."

"Hey guys, check this out," Gus interrupted. He had fallen behind the group and stopped. He pointed at a poster taped to a nearby door.

"What is it?" Mikey asked, joining him.

"'Bad Dad Club,'" Gus read, "'Meeting tonight at 7 PM. Bar is closed due to meeting.'"

"Bad Dad Club? What's that?"

"Um, it doesn't say," Art answered, scanning the poster. "It just says to stop by if you're interested and stay if you want."

"That's rather blasé," Gus mumbled.

"What does that even mean?" Art asked.

"Basically it means disinterested. Apathetic."

"Ah, that makes sense," Art replied. "Why didn't you just say that?" Gus shrugged.

"But it intrigues me nonetheless," Mikey mused. "Almost like it's deliberately vague to pique our interest. Silly marketing ploys."

"Silly marketing," Neil agreed. "So do we want to come back? At least to see what this Club is all about?"

"I think I do," Art answered. "Given that Father's Day is the day after tomorrow, I don't think the meeting is a coincidence."

"True," Gus said. "Plus it has to be pretty impressive if a bar is closing to host it."

"So let's come back!" Mikey decided. "If we like what's going on, we can stay! If not, oh darn, back to Netflix and video games!"

"Well, I'll set a reminder in my phone," Gus said, reaching into his pocket. "Let's get back to the hotel and order some lunch. I want something more than Lunchables and fast food."

23

A bell chimed as Neil opened the door and followed his friends into the bar. The room was dim and empty.

"Are we too early?" Mikey asked, pulling out his phone.

"Barely," Gus answered. "The poster said that it starts at 7, and it's just a few minutes until now. Maybe the meeting is in a back room."

"Or in a basement," Art added. "Let's take a look around."

"That won't be necessary" a voice said suddenly. The boys turned their attention to the far side of the room, where a woman appeared behind the bar. She was strongly built with dark skin and hair, pulled back in a high ponytail. She wore dark jeans with a white tank top that showed off her sculpted, tattooed arms.

"Oh, hi," Neil greeted. "We're, uh, here for the meeting?"

"Is that a question or a statement?" she replied dryly. Neil glanced awkwardly at his friends. After a moment, the woman busted out laughing. "Oh you boys need to lighten up. The meetings are serious enough." She hoisted herself onto the bar and spun around to face the guys.

"Well if you weren't the most intimidating woman I've ever met…" Neil mumbled.

"Ignore him," Mikey interrupted, approaching the woman. "I'm Mikey, by the way. This bozo is Neil, and these guys are Gus and Art."

"Nice to meet ya," she replied, shaking their hands. "I'm Alex. And this, as I'm sure you know, is my bar, Drunken Respite. If you're still planning on participating in the meeting, follow me."

"So what is the Bad Dad Club?" Art asked, following Alex to a staircase in a back room.

"Um, simply put, it's a support group for people with daddy issues," she explained. "That's all you really need to know coming in. You'll figure out the rest through the introductory group."

"The introductory group?" Mikey repeated. "Is there a veteran group?"

"Yea. We start in the basement for some socializing time before splitting up. The regular members go upstairs to talk, while the newbies stay down here. But that's enough explanation.

Check it out for yourself." Alex opened the door at the bottom of the stairs and gestured for the guys to enter.

A couple dozen people milled around the room, hardly talking to each other. A table sat along the far wall, covered in various snack and drink options. A cork board labeled 'Hall of Fame' hung on a wall, and chairs lined the walls.

"Hello! Welcome to the Bad Dad Club!" A stout man in cargo shorts and a graphic tee approached the group and extended his hand. "My name is Brandon. I'm in charge of the introductory group this week."

"So what's the plan for the night, then?" Art asked after the guys introduced themselves.

"Um," Brandon stammered, glancing at Alex. "I think we'll start the meeting around 7:15, so you can take some time to meet the other folks and grab a bite to eat. Go on!" He shooed them away and turned to talk to Alex.

"Well, uh, we're here," Neil said, scanning the room.

"What should we do?" Gus asked. "What do you want to do?"

"I want to stay," Art replied. "I want to learn as much as I can about this group. See what it does and how it does it. Hopefully it's more than just a pity party."

"I don't know about you guys," Neil interrupted, "but I'm getting that redhead's number."

"Manchester!" Gus shouted, cackling. Art and Mikey cheered and exchanged high fives with him as Neil shook his head.

"I hope you're ready to lose this game, Gussie," Neil taunted. "You forget that I'm the smoothest one here!"

"So smooth that women slip right through your fingers," Gus retorted. "You're all bark and no bite, bro. We all know it."

"Oh just you wait and see. I'll have her number before the end of the night. I have a plan. But until then, I think that snack bar is calling my name. Mikey, I need my wingman!"

"Uh sure?" Mikey replied, perplexed.

"Think he'll succeed?" Art asked as Neil and Mikey walked away.

"Not a chance," Gus said. "I have a plan of my own. Let's go mingle with the folks until the groups separate."

"Are you going to tell me your plan?"

"Well if we can get out of Neil's line of sight, you can bear witness to my genius."

"Sweet! Let's casually head her direction and wait for him to turn around," Art suggested, watching Neil as they crossed the room. "Alright, now, he's not looking!"

"Excuse me," Gus said, tapping the young woman on the shoulder.

"Whoa!" She jumped as she turned around before busting out laughing. "Sorry, you startled me! I'm Jordan, nice to meet you."

"I'm Gus, and this is my buddy Art. This is gonna be super awkward, so I'm gonna be straightforward with you. I need a favor."

"Okay?" she said slowly. "What's the favor?"

"Well at the snack bar is a guy in a V-neck and beanie. His name is Neil. He's another friend. Long story short, he plans to ask you for your number by the end of the night. If he succeeds, he wins a little game that he and I are playing right now and gets to smack me in the face. If he fails, I win and get to slap him. So I need you to give him a number that isn't yours when he comes over."

"Oh," Jordan said, pausing. "You're right, that is kinda awkward. I'm not sure how I feel about a game being played about getting my number."

"Fair enough," Gus agreed. "But if I win, no-body gets your number! So what do you say? Are you in?"

"Hmm, maybe. Whose number should I give him then?"

"Give him one of ours!" Art replied. "Then we can make him call it and tease him when our phone rings!"

"That's genius!" Gus exclaimed, high-fiving Art. "We'll catfish him so hard!."

"That does sound funny," Jordan agreed, grinning slightly. "Alright, I'm in on two conditions. First, you get a video of him calling the number, realizing he's been duped, and getting slapped. I want to see it all."

"Deal," Art replied quickly. "I can take care of all of that."

"Perfect. Second, you have to teach me this game that you're playing. It sounds like it could be a lot of fun."

"Oh definitely! It's unpredictable, but it's fun as long as you don't take it too seriously," Gus explained. "How am I going to teach you though?"

"Well, how do you think?" Jordan asked, raising an eyebrow at him.

"Give her your phone," Art whispered loudly, elbowing him.

"I figured that out myself, thanks." Gus pulled out his phone, opened his contacts, and handed it to Jordan. "I'll text you with my name so you have my number. Then you can memorize it for the night and put it in Neil's phone."

"Perfect!" Jordan said, handing the phone back. "I look forward to—"

"Excuse me! Um, everybody!" Gus and Art turned to the doorway and saw Brandon standing on a chair. "May I, uh, have your attention please? It's, uh, time for club to start! Please head upstairs if you're a returning attendee. If not, you'll, um, circle up here in this room. Thank you!"

"Well I guess I'll talk to you later! I have to head upstairs. Are you guys coming? Or—"

"Well technically it's only our first visit," Gus replied. "So we should stay down here."

"Let's ask Brandon if we're allowed to skip the intro group," Art suggested. "I may stay down here, but maybe like you and Neil can go up."

"Good idea! I knew I kept you around for a reason!" Gus laughed and patted Art on the head. "I'll grab Neil and see you up there, Jordan!"

Jordan nodded and walked away. Gus and Art meandered through the dispersing crowd to Mikey and Neil.

"Bro!" Gus exclaimed, shaking Neil by the shoulders. "Red went upstairs! You better go get her, tiger!"

"What? Are you serious? I have to go up there too!" Without another word, Neil started weaving toward the stairs.

"Yo, I'm coming too!" Gus shouted, following him. "I have to make sure you don't cheat!"

"Well I guess that leaves us to scope out the intro group," Mikey said, looking around for a chair. "Unless you want to follow them?"

"Nah," Art replied, shrugging. "Gus has a plan. It'll be fine. Besides, I'm curious about the group's purpose and function. I'm staying."

"Works for me."

"And it works out perfectly. We can tell Gus and Neil about this part of the club later, and they can fill us in on the other group."

"Clever girl!" Mikey said. "We should take a seat. I think we're about to start." The two found seats near the snack bar just as Alex stepped into the middle of the circle.

"Good evening! I'm glad you all could make it to this month's meeting of the Bad Dad Club! If I didn't meet you already, my name is Alex, and I'm in charge of the downstairs group. Feel free to get up and enjoy the snacks and drinks through-out the rest of the night. But without further ado, let's get started!"

24

"To start off, let's play a little game!" Alex proclaimed. "It's called Who the Heck Are Ya! The rules are simple: we'll go around in a circle and give our first name, our age, and the superpower that we wish we could have. I'll go first! My name is Alex, I'm 43, and I would choose the power of teleportation. Who wouldn't want to avoid Chicago rush hour?" The group laughed as she retrieved a chair and joined the circle. She motioned to the woman on her left to continue.

"Oh, um," she mumbled. "I'm Kirstin. Thirty years old. And, um, I think I would like the power to fly. Is, uh, is that everything?" She stared at the floor and fidgeted with the hem of her vest.

"I guess it's my turn then. The name's Sullivan, but everyone calls me Sulley. Age 50. I would gladly take some kind of regeneration power, like Hugh Jackman in those comic book movies. I'm getting to that age where everything aches, and I would like to keep putting up sky-scrapers for a while longer." Sulley chuckled and crossed his arms across his chest.

"Dillon. 22. Super strength so I can beat the shit out of anybody who doesn't leave me alone." She shot a glance at Mikey. "Your turn."

"If you insist," he agreed. "Hiya, I'm Mikey, age 22 as well. I would definitely choose super speed. I could get so much more stuff done. Plus, who wouldn't like bragging about being the fastest man alive?"

"Well then," Art mumbled. "Um, my friends call me Art. I'm 21 years old. I would love the power to enter any movie, TV show, or video game. That would be a lot of fun."

"That does sound intriguing," Art's neighbor said. She brushed her bleach blonde hair behind her ear. "I'm Andrea. Twenty-six years old. The power to heal myself and others. As a nurse, that would make my job infinitely easier!"

"Oh Andrea. I think I'd have to agree with Flowers over there and take super strength."

"It's Dillon, not Flowers." She glared across the circle at the dark-haired girl.

"Sorry," she said quickly. "I didn't remember your name. It was meant to be a compliment. I do like your tattoos and your leggings. Anyway, I'm supposed to tell my name or something? It's Sara, and I'm 28. Your turn, Dani."

"No it's fine, just introduce me," Dani retorted sarcastically, rolling her eyes. "Care to answer the other questions for me while you're at it?"

"Of course! She's clearly fifty, and she wants to become some kind of Ice Woman."

"You're so stupid." Dani punched Sara on the arm and shook her head. "I'm only twenty-five. Though, ice powers would be pretty legit, especially if they made me immune to the wind and cold here in Chicago. And as a bonus, I could be a sexy badass like Danielle Panabaker!"

"That just leaves me. I'm Christian. Thirty-eight years old. And I've always wanted to be able to shoot lightning. It may not be very practical or safe, but you can't even argue that it wouldn't be cool! Also being able to zap stupid mosquitoes would be handy."

"Very good everybody," Alex said. "Now that we've had some laughs and gotten to know each other, let's get down to business."

"Finally," Dillon interjected. "I'm ready to murder the fuck out of some Huns."

"Well what you do outside of the Bad Dad Club is none of my concern," Alex replied. "Maybe you'll even make a friend or two who would, uh, help you with that. But anyway, let's get this meeting started."

"Let me guess," Sara interrupted, standing up. "Hi, I'm Sara, and I have daddy issues." She curtsied before sitting down.

"Well, I was going to open the floor for anybody who wanted to share about why you came here," Alex explained. "Everybody can share, or nobody. But keep it short. Tell us which parent brought you here and what he or she did."

"Wait, we can talk about our mothers?" Sara asked. "I honestly didn't really expect the Bad Dad Club to be open to that."

"This group may have started to help people with father issues, but mother issues are fairly common and equally traumatic. So when the group became a more official support system, I naturally opened it up to anybody and everybody who wants help."

"That's pretty cool. I guess I'll tell you about my mother then. Long story short, she went to jail for some drug charges when I was young. I tried to visit her with my dad, but she refused to see us. Then she got out and disappeared. I think I was eight when she went to prison, so I guess it's been twenty years since I last saw her."

"Thank you for sharing Sara. Anybody else?"

"Um," Mikey said after a moment, "my story isn't nearly as dramatic bu—"

"Hold on," Alex held up her hand and locked eyes with him. "We have a single rule here at the Bad Dad Club: never devalue someone's story. Not even your own. All of you are likely here because of real pain caused by a real person. Your pain is just as real as Sara's, or anybody else's for that matter. Just because your scar is in a different place doesn't mean that it hurts any less. It just hurts different parts of you."

"Oh," Mikey mumbled. "That's a good point. So, um, my story is different from—Sara, wasn't it—Sara's, yea. My parents are still together, so I haven't had to deal with either of them leaving. But both of them, especially my father, have put constant pressure on me to act older and more mature than I am. Such as forcing me to get my younger siblings to school on time and to work in all my free time to pay for my car and my clothes and anything else I wanted or even needed. But those are all details for another time."

"Much better. Thank you for sharing, Mikey. Last call for any other takers. Going once. Going twice. Okay, moving on! Now it's time for a brief monologue." Alex stood up and crossed the room to stand in front of the bulletin board.

"The Bad Dad Club began as a sort of Alcoholics Anonymous for people with father issues. It serves as a place where people can come together and learn to cope with whatever issues they may have. The mission statement for the group is here on the board: 'The Bad Dad Club exists to connect orphaned individuals with other orphaned individuals to share experience, strength, and hope for coping and recovery.' I think it's quite self-explanatory, so this is where I stop and open the floor for questions." Alex clasped her hands and scanned the room.

"Define 'orphan,'" Sulley asked.

"For our group, it means anybody with a grievance against a parent. We define it broadly because we understand that even the most overtly healthy families have problems. We want everyone to come here and be included, regardless of how — oh what's the right word — minimal the complaint may be.

"Put another way, this isn't a club just for people with dead dads or with deadbeat, absent, or abusive dads. It's for people with mom issues too, and it include all the various parent-related grievances. I hesitate to give examples, because that could suggest that your situation isn't as severe as your neighbor's, when it could be your worst-case scenario. Does that make sense?"

"Yea, it does. That's an interesting approach," Sulley replied. "I like it. Though being so broad may overextend your group's responsibilities."

"That is true," Alex agreed. "But you're all here, aren't you? We had a good number of folks here tonight, and, spoilers, there are more than just two of us running this circus." She grinned slyly and winked at Sulley.

"How did the club start?" Art asked after a moment of silence. "Where did you get the idea, and how did it develop into what it is today?"

"Funny story about that," Alex began, chuckling. "It started back when I was in college. My friends and I regularly made jokes about our fathers being absent or being terrible. I don't remember the specifics, but at some point, I think we made a joke around someone who was new to the group. When they asked why we made such jokes, someone responded that we were basically a club of people with bad dads. Then someone sarcastically suggested making it a real group, and my roommate went on AOL and created a chatroom. She added all of us to it. Then every Father's Day, we would talk and share memes and videos and articles about absent fathers as a weird way to cope.

"Over the years, we graduated, moved away, and made new friends. Father's Day would come around, and our new friends would mention their dad issues. So we each added new people to the group as they revealed themselves, which led to the group growing. One year, my friends came to visit me here in Chicago in mid-June, so we hit up this bar to have some drinks, reminisce, and crack jokes. The bartender found out why we were there and invited us to mingle with the other drinkers and hear their stories, then suggested that we come back the following year. That was the routine for a few years before someone had the idea to make it an official group, so we researched how to start a support group, made flyers, and held our first meeting. It's grown a lot since then, but that's how it started."

"Interesting. And do your friends still come to visit?" Dani asked.

"One or two of them will visit every couple years. But we usually get together around Thanksgiving, and most of them have their own Bad Dad Clubs to lead," Alex answered.

"That's cool!" Sulley exclaimed. "So could we start our own clubs?"

"Absolutely! That's actually something that we encourage regular members to do. Or, if you're only in town this weekend, we advise you to connect with the group—you know, exchange phone numbers and Facebook info—so that you can continue to learn about the club and start one wherever you call home. All we ask is that you maintain the same mission, values, and covenant that we use here."

"Covenant?" Dillon interrupted. "There's a covenant?"

"Yes, there is. That's the last thing that I want to discuss tonight, so if there aren't any more questions"—Alex paused and scanned the room—"then I'll tell you about it." She grabbed a stack of papers from a nearby table and walked around the circle, handing one to each person.

"This is your covenant here at the Bad Dad Club," she explained. "It explains our core values, our mission statement, and how we function as a support group. There are two lines at the bottom for signatures. One is for you to signify that you commit to pursuing and upholding these values in these meetings and in your day-to-day life. The other is for your accountability partner. This is the person whom you choose to help you with this covenant. It could be someone in this room, or it could be someone on the other side of the world. Just make sure it's someone who knows you well and someone you talk to regularly."

"So, do we have to, like, sign this and return it?" Dillon asked hesitantly.

"Absolutely not," Alex said. "This is for you. The covenant is intended to remind you of the club when you're not here. I encourage you to sign it and put it somewhere that you'll see regularly. Hang it above your desk, laminate it and tape it to your bathroom mirror, put it in your underwear drawer. But we don't want it back.

"One last thing. I know this all seems super formal and official, but don't treat it that way. We have core values and principles and guidelines for a reason, but they aren't intended to take over your life. Just be supportive of each other. Do unto others, y'know?"

"Question," Dillon added. "What's this box on the side of the page?"

"Ah, that is an important part of the covenant. Good eye. One of the key tenets of any support group is that the individual lacks the strength necessary to overcome her issues by herself. So that box is your source of power. For example, my source of strength is my Lord and Savior Jesus Christ. But it could also be your spouse, your child, or your accountability partner. We recommend putting their name in that box to remind you to seek their strength, especially when times are hard."

"That makes sense," Sulley said. "Is there anything else?"

"Nope! You're free to mingle, enjoy our snacks and refreshments, or leave. And if you have any more questions, feel free to come ask! And I, and everyone else involved, hope you come back to the Bad Dad Club!"

25

Gus and Neil followed Brandon upstairs to the main room of the bar. When they entered the room, they saw a handful of people waiting for them. Jordan leaned against a pool table across the room, arms crossed in front of her chest.

Neil immediately approached the table and found a pool cue in the corner. "Who wants to play?" he asked, looking first at Jordan before scanning the room eagerly.

"Sure, I'm in," Jordan said, shrugging.

"I'm always down to destroy you at billiards," Gus teased. "Anybody else want to play? No? Then I guess we'll play cutthroat. Neil, you rack the balls."

"Way to make yourselves at home," Brandon said, approaching the pool table. "Gather around everyone, we're getting a free show! Anybody want to place some bets?"

"Ten bucks on Curly!" a peppy blonde

woman exclaimed, pulling up a stool.

"Then I'll put ten on Jordan," a woman with dreadlocks said.

"Anybody else?" Brandon asked, glancing around the room. "All right, I'll put ten on the hipster since nobody else will!"

"Wow, thanks for the pity bet," Neil grumbled. "You're a lot more lively now than a moment ago! You barely managed to get our attention to bring us up here, and now you're running a gambling ring?"

Brandon laughed and shook his head. "Crowds aren't my thing. Neither is anything formal or official. But playing a game of pool and talking about life? That's my jam."

"Okay, I'm breaking!" Jordan said, leaning over the pool table. "I'm ready to win this game. Does the winner get some of the winnings?"

"Of course!" Brandon agreed. "Are you playing with the scratch rule? Depending on how bad these guys are, we might be here all night!"

"If we don't, Neil doesn't stand a chance," Gus replied, sticking his tongue out at his friend. "Let's use it. If it's a problem, we'll get rid of it later." Nodding, Jordan aimed and shot the cue ball across the table, scattering the pool balls.

"Well now that the game's started, let's start

this meeting," Brandon said. "We'll begin with introductions. Hipster, you first, then we'll go clockwise around the room."

"As long as you stop calling me 'Hipster.'" Neil took a shot and knocked a ball into a pocket. "My name is Neil, and I'm playing balls 1 through 5." He smirked at Gus and lined up another shot.

"Pretty much everybody here already knows me, but I'm Jordan!"

"My turn? I'm Mikayla." Gus looked up to see a black-haired woman throwing darts nearby, seemingly disinterested in the group.

"Hello! My name is Taylor!" the peppy blonde said, grinning broadly. "Glad you all could make it tonight!"

"I hope you all know me, but if not, I'm Brandon." He gave a small wave.

"Call me Nicole," the woman with dreadlocks said dryly.

"Sara," a short woman in a hoodie mumbled.

Gus sunk a pool ball into the corner pocket. "Everybody calls me Gus. And I'm playing 11 through 15. Your turn, Jordan."

"Good. Well, except I forgot to mention one little thing. We have a sort of tradition here at the Bad Dad Club: all new members of this group have to say something positive about a parent."

The group turned to look at Gus and Neil as Mikayla continued to ignore them.

"What?" Gus responded. "Why?"

"If you find reasons to like someone, it becomes more difficult to hate them," Jordan said. "At least, that's what we're always told."

"I mean, if you think about it logically, it makes sense," Nicole added. "If you vilify your mom or dad for whatever reason, you find more and more reasons to hate him or her. But if you say something good about your mom, you force yourself to like her, if only for a moment. It's a start of a new habit."

"Good, good!" Brandon agreed. "I'm glad you've been paying attention. We do it to illustrate a point about the BDC. I'll go into that more after you guys say something."

"Wait, just us?" Neil looked at Gus then Brandon, confused.

"Yea, just you two," Sara said quietly. "We've all been here before and done it."

"I guess I'll go first," Gus volunteered. "Last I knew, Brock was an amazing baker. Every Christmas, he would bake like a hundred dozen cookies from scratch and deliver them to friends and family. I helped him bake a few times and always ate way too many cookies."

"That's awesome!" Taylor exclaimed. "Do you bake? Did you bring us cookies?"

"Oh, um," Gus stammered, averting his eyes. "I've baked a couple times. I'm not as good as Brock was though. But no, I didn't bring any cookies. Sorry to get your hopes up."

"Darn!" she replied. "Maybe next time! If I ever see you outside of Club, I expect some cookies, Gus!" She laughed heartily.

"Okay, sure! Sounds like a deal!"

"I got it!" Neil interrupted. "I have my thing. I can't believe I didn't think of this sooner. My dad taught me to play guitar. That's probably what sparked my love of music, and I hope to make a living by producing music one day."

"So if we pulled out a guitar, could you play us a little something?" Nicole asked. "There's probably one somewhere in this place."

"That would be cool to see," Brandon agreed. "Maybe we'll poke around after we talk some more. But that's good, guys. I don't know your relationships with your dads, but that right there was a step forward. Maybe you'll have ten more steps tonight, maybe you'll be taking steps the rest of your life. But all that matters now is that you've taken at least one step."

"Interesting," Neil mused. "So why did we

have to do it? Something about illustrating a point about this group?"

"Yes, that. Who knows the mission statement for the Bad Dad Club?" Brandon scanned the room slowly. "Sara? Mikayla?"

"Pass," Sara grumbled. Mikayla said nothing and continued throwing darts.

"Okay, that's fine." Brandon looked at Nicole and then Taylor. "What about you?"

"'The Bad Dad Club exists to connect orphaned individuals with other orphaned individuals to share experience, strength, and hope for coping and recovery,'" Nicole recited. "Basically, they want us to get to know each other outside of here. They want us to talk, hang out, encourage one another, whatever."

"You're exactly right! The goal of the Bad Dad Club is life transformation. We want to create an environment and facilitate relationships that promote healthy living. Or, at the risk of oversimplifying, we want you to help each other and yourselves to forgive your parents."

"Wait," Neil said, turning to Gus. "That sounds like what Art is studying."

"Yea, it's called 'counseling,' buddy," he replied dryly.

"These guys are pretty clever," Taylor noted.

"Well, I'm a quick learner," Gus explained. "It helps that my roommate for the last three years is a psychology major. Neil must've learned a thing or two from exposure." Gus shrugged as Neil feigned swinging his pool cue at him.

"You're both right," Brandon said. "It is counseling. That tends to be a misunderstood trigger word, especially for guys. People think it means sitting down and talking about your feelings with a stranger. While that can be part of counseling, that's not the whole truth. The goal is equipping the 'client' with the skills to handle his or her own problems."

"So you're saying we don't actually have to talk?" Neil asked. "Like when you asked us to say something nice about our dads?"

"Just saying, I've been here for months and haven't said anything about myself," Mikayla interrupted. "None of that lovey-dovey feeling nonsense for me. I just show up for the food."

"I would have insisted that you do at least that, Neil, but you're correct. Mikayla is a perfect example. She introduced herself when asked, and she said something good about her parent. But other than that, she mostly just provides snarky commentary for us."

"Oh you all love it," she replied. "This club

would be so boring without me."

"Yes, yes we do," Brandon agreed, chuckling. "Anyway, the goal is life change. We want you to lead a healthier life. So we do things to challenge the way that you think and feel about your parents, such as saying something positive about them. The hope is that these things lead to some degree of catharsis so that your future can be free of your past."

"That sounds good and all, but how do you know it works?" Gus asked skeptically.

"You know, there once was a time in my life when I hated my father and I lived for my own glory," Brandon said after a brief pause. "But then God forgave me through Jesus Christ and I chose to follow Him. Now, I've forgiven my father and committed to living for Jesus's glory. Do you have a story like that?"

"Wait, what?" Neil looked up confused and barely nicked the cue ball. "Dang it! Any chance I can retry that shot?"

"Nope!" Jordan teased. "That's what you get for being distracted like a scrub!"

"Fine," Neil said. "Anyway, what does that have to do with anything? I asked how you know this club works, not what your personal testimony is."

"Well they're one and the same," Brandon answered. "Everybody has a story like that. Every story has three components: action, choice, and reaction. The action is what happens to and around you. The choice is how you decide to respond to the action. And the reaction is the result of your choice."

"For example," Mikayla interrupted, "the action could be my mom hitting me for being out past curfew. I can choose to hit her back, and the result is spending my high school years in juvie."

"Exactly. Any component could be good or bad, but each depends upon the previous part. And your choice can change at any time. For me, my father was never around when I was a kid. I never met him. So for years I hated him, wanted to track him down and yell and punch him for ditching me. But then Jesus got a hold of me, and I slowly came to a place of forgiveness. I realized that my father was someone broken and in need of a Healer and Savior, just like me. I stopped thinking of him as the villain in my life and started viewing him as the hero in his own life. That's my story." Brandon paused and looked at each person in the room. "Do any of you want to share something about yourselves?"

"Um," Sara began, "my dad was a, uh, hard-core alcoholic. And, um, when I got older, um, I decided not to drink. Ever. Um because I didn't want to...become that kind of person."

"Very good Sara. Thanks for sharing. Anybody else?"

"I wrote my letter," Taylor said. She dug a neatly folded envelope out of her purse and began to fidget with it.

"What are you going to do with it?" Brandon asked. "Have you decided?"

"Um," she replied slowly, "no. I don't know. I think I'll just keep it in my purse until I decide what to do. Maybe I'll take it out and talk to my mom when I visit her over the holidays."

"That might be worth considering," Brandon said serenely. "Whatever you do, we're proud of you for writing it." He applauded Taylor briefly, and everyone in the room joined.

"Wait, what's so important about the letter?" Gus asked.

"I'll tell you when I finish my spiel about your story," Brandon said. "Or maybe I'll let Taylor handle it. Anyway, like I said earlier, the goal here at Bad Dad Club is life change. We want you to look back on what has happened to you and be empowered to make a wise choice to change your life for the better. Whatever happened with your fathers or mothers does not define you; how you react and behave as a result does."

"Oh. But you specifically mentioned Jesus as being your 'empowerment' earlier. Are you trying to convert us all?" Neil asked.

Brandon laughed heartily. "Well yes and no. Your source of motivation could be anything outside of yourself. It could be Gus. That's for you to determine. I just never miss a chance to tell someone about Jesus."

"That makes sense," Neil replied. "Wait, am I even still in this game? Jordan, Gus, what the heck? When did I get out?"

"Finally he notices!" Gus taunted, laughing. "You've been out for a minute or so. You just got so distracted by Brandon and Taylor talking."

"Well you're lucky I wasn't focused. I would've lasted a bit longer," Neil mumbled. "I hope Jordan wins."

"Well we'll keep playing until either someone wins or the meeting is over," Gus said. "Speaking of, are we going to do any official meeting business, or is everything super casual?"

"Define 'official meeting business,'" Brandon replied. "There's never anything official. We show up, we chat about life, we provide counseling and encouragement as needed. Sometimes we meet for half an hour, sometimes we're here all night. The Bad Dad Club exists to serve its members, not to further its own agenda. I have nothing to add, so you're free to hang out or leave." Brandon stood up and approached the dart board.

"Wait!" Taylor exclaimed. "Were you serious about me explaining the letters to Gus and Neil?"

"Absolutely," Brandon answered. "You know what the task is. Grab them each an envelope."

Taylor sighed and left the room. She returned and approached the pool table with two envelopes in hand. She handed them to Gus and Neil.

"The assignment is to write a letter to your parent," she explained. "Not one of hatred and anger, but one of compassion and forgiveness. Kind of like when you said something nice about your dads earlier. But also don't lie. Be honest."

"Ugh I thought I was done with homework," Gus groaned sarcastically. "When's it due? How many words do you want?"

"Very funny," Taylor said, rolling her eyes and fighting back a grin. "Write it when you're ready. Make it as long or short as it needs to be."

"Then what do we do with it?" Gus asked.

"Well if you wouldn't interrupt, I'd tell you!"

she replied sassily, putting her hand on her hip. "Do whatever you want. Mine's sitting in my purse. I think Mikayla threw darts at hers and then burned it. Brandon mailed his to his father. A bunch are nailed to the bulletin board downstairs. The instructions are vague so that you handle your emotions and thoughts on your own. So you do you." Taylor winked at the guys and joined Brandon and Mikayla at the dart board.

"Hey schmucks!" Mikey yelled from across the room. Gus and Neil turned to see him and Art heading for the exit. "Let's get out of here!"

"Okay, you win, Jordan! Good game! Bye guys! Thanks for letting us stay!" Gus waved and followed his friends outside, tucking the envelope into his back pocket. Neil stopped to talk to Jordan before hurrying after them.

26

A couple of days passed before Mikey and Gus loaded their belongings into the SUV and left the hotel to fuel up and restock on snacks and drinks. Neil and Art woke up and packed their suitcases by the time they returned. The group grabbed some fast food burgers and fries for lunch and hit the road for Springfield.

"How far is Springfield from here?" Gus asked. "Three and a half hours?"

"Something like that," Mikey answered. "I bet I could make it in three or less."

"I'll take that bet!" Neil exclaimed. "Loser buys D'Arcy's for everyone."

"Deal! I hope you're ready to put your money where your mouth is!" Mikey reached into the backseat and shook Neil's hand. He then pressed the accelerator to the floor.

"Okay, before anything else distracts us," Gus began, turning to Neil, "someone has a phone call to make!" Art and Mikey started cheering in agreement.

"Well if you insist!" Neil reached into his pocket and pulled out his phone.

"Art, get this on video!" Mikey exclaimed.

"Good idea! Don't call until I tell you to! Ready? 3, 2, 1, go!"

Neil tapped the screen on his phone and raised it to his ear, grinning eagerly. Art panned the camera to catch Mikey and Gus's reactions.

"Wait, what's this?" Gus asked, reaching into his pocket. "Weird. Nobody ever calls me." He raised his phone to his ear.

"Hello? Is this Jordan?" Neil asked.

"Jordan," Gus repeated slowly. "Jordan. Jordan. Do I know a Jordan? Hey Mikey, do we know of a Jordan?" Art and Mikey busted out laughing.

"What?" Neil lowered his phone and looked at Gus, dumbfounded. "When? How? Why?"

"Who is it?" Mikey asked.

"It's Neil. He's asking for someone named Jordan! Do we know of anybody by that name?"

"Wait, is Jordan a guy or a girl?" Art added.

"Guys! What the hell?" Neil exclaimed.

"Neil, is this Jordan a guy or a girl?" Gus asked into the phone.

"Shut up! I'm hanging up now!" Neil dropped his phone to the floor and punched Gus in the arm. "I hate you guys! How did this happen?"

"Oh, he hung up," Gus said dejectedly. "I guess he didn't want to talk to Jordan that badly after all." He shrugged and set his phone on the dashboard.

"Gus! Explain! Before I jump up there and throw you out of this car!"

"Well, you saw her and said you'd get her number," Art began. "Gus Manchestered you. Then you went to the snack bar with Mikey."

"That's right! I did Manchester him! Come here, loser!" Gus reached into the backseat and slapped Neil on the cheek. "I win! Anyway, that's when I made my move. I gave her my number to give to you and got her number to send her the video of you trying to call her. Which reminds me. Art, send it to me!"

"Who do you think I am?" he replied. "I already sent it."

"Perfect! Time to send it to Jordan! Want me to say 'hi' for you, Neil?"

"Just you wait, Gus Millburn," Neil warned. "Vengeance will be mine."

"Ooh I'm shaking in my Converse," Gus said sarcastically.

"All right, now that the shenanigans are over, time for some jams!" Mikey tuned the radio to an early 2000s station and turned up the volume.

"Hey look, the windmills!" Neil exclaimed, pointing out the window.

"Technically, they're wind turbines," Gus corrected. Scattered throughout the land around them, the guys saw dozens of wind turbines rotating in the wind.

"Dude, nobody cares!" Neil smacked him in the arm. Gus retaliated by throwing an empty can of Dr. Pepper at him.

"You know what's unnerving?" Mikey asked. "Imagine driving down this interstate in the middle of the night. There's no light except from the cars around you, so it's total darkness. But then you look to the side and see a ton of red lights above the horizon, blinking slowly. It's so eerie. You feel like you're about to drive into hell or something. Not that I'm speaking from experience or anything."

"That sounds kind of creepy," Gus agreed. "I can see the lights and how the blades make them seem to blink. I can only imagine what it would be like if these dozens of lights were all you saw. Good thing it's daytime."

"It's weird how small they seem," Art noted.

"They look small, but then there we drive by the ones that are closer to the road and see that they're like 300 feet tall."

"Imagine being one of the engineers," Mikey added. "They have to climb up on those things and fix them. How would you like being an engineer, Gus?"

"Um, how about no? I would rather do almost *anything* else than work on top of one of those turbines. I don't like climbing a ten-foot ladder, let alone a 300-foot turbine."

"You're no fun, dude!" Neil taunted.

"Sorry I'm not a fan of dying!"

"How much longer until we get to Springfield?" Art interrupted.

"Um, probably about an hour. We're making really good time." Mikey glanced at Neil quickly. "I hope you're ready to pay up, bro! I might have to order a second horseshoe!"

Neil rolled his eyes as they continued down the interstate. True to his estimate, they turned off I-55 to enter Springfield about an hour later. When they pulled into the parking lot at D'Arcy's Pint, barely two and a half hours had passed since they left Chicago.

"Dang it. That's twice now that I've ended up paying for our meals," Neil muttered. "Well a deal's a deal. Food's on me. But don't be jerks."

"Us, jerks? Never!" Art replied. "Just ask Jordan! Oh wait." Neil glared at him.

Laughing, they stepped into the restaurant to wait for an open table. As they followed a gothic young waitress named Maribelle to their table, Gus noticed that many tables seemed to be occupied by fathers with their sons. The guys had been there enough to know exactly what they wanted, so they ordered immediately.

"This place is pretty busy," Neil noted. "Seems like a lot of dads and their kids. And then there's us."

"We should probably talk about that," Gus said. "What are we going to do about our dads? Now seems like a good time to do something, after visiting the Bad Dad Club."

The table fell quiet. The guys sipped on Mountain Dew and fiddled with the silverware to avoid answering. A few moments passed before anybody spoke.

"I think first we have to figure out what to do with our letters," Neil said. "I haven't written mine yet, but I know exactly what I'll say. What about you guys?"

"I actually already did something like that," Art replied. "It was for my counseling class last year. We basically had to think of the worst event to happen to us and write about what happened, how it affected us emotionally, and what we've done to cope with it. I picked my dad's overbearing parenting, so like Neil, I know more or less what I'd say."

"Same," Mikey added. "I've talked about it enough with the three of you that writing it down will be easy. I just have to, you know, do it."

"Well you're all beating me," Gus admitted. "I don't even know what to say."

"Oh!" Neil yelled, drawing looks from nearby tables. "For once we're farther on an assignment than Gus!" The table laughed for a moment.

"I'll figure it out," Gus mumbled, stirring his drink absently. "In the meantime, what are we going to do?" Conversation paused as Maribelle returned with refills.

"Here you go guys," she said. "Your food should be ready before too long." She smiled sweetly and walked away.

"She's cute," Art commented. "Are you going to get her number too, Neil?"

"Haha," he replied dryly. "I'm never going to live that down, am I?"

"Not a chance!" Gus exclaimed. "Jordan thought it was hilarious!"

Mikey chuckled. "Anyway, getting us back on track, I think I need to talk to my dad. I'm not sure if he knows how much he's messed me up. He and I have never talk about anything personal like that. It's just him telling me to babysit and me updating him on school, Amber, and stuff. Maybe telling him what's up will help us get along. We don't even need to get along as father and son. I'd be fine with a mature, adult relationship. Thoughts?"

"It's worth a shot," Neil agreed. "At least you can vent to him. Get all that stuff off your chest so that you can process it and move forward. Plus you're moving out, so you don't have to worry about him becoming awkward or resentful and making your life miserable."

"That's a good point. Venting is fairly healthy," Art added. "Keeping all of that crap inside of you isn't good. It affects your mental and emotional health. But simply talking about whatever's wrong is useful, even if the circumstances don't change. Tons of people go to the counseling center on campus just to rant about life. Often, they solve their own problems as they express them, with minimal help from the counselors."

"Gus, what do you think?" Mikey asked.

"I agree with Art and Neil. But you have to be

ready for the unexpected. With all the stuff that's built up, you may end up yelling and screaming at him, and he could react the same way. And it may change nothing about your relationship. But I think you should do it, for your own sake."

"Yea, that makes sense." Mikey paused to take a drink. "Too bad we didn't talk about this earlier. We could've stopped by my house while we were in the Chicago area."

"Maybe we'll end up back in the area before this trip ends," Neil suggested. "Or you can talk to him when you go home, before moving down to Tennessee."

"I could do that. That would give me some time to organize my thoughts and feelings."

"How are you doing?" Maribelle asked, returning to the table. "What brings a group of handsome young men such as yourselves here?" She smiled sweetly and winked at Neil.

"Someone wants a good tip," he replied confidently. "Luckily for her, we tip well regardless of how our server looks or acts."

"Well damn, I guess you guys know the game as well as I do," she said, deadpanning.

"Way to go, Neil, you ruined her day!" Gus said, throwing his straw wrapper at Neil.

"Yea, Neil," she echoed, shooting him a disgruntled look. "I could've been funny and flirty. Instead you get the everyday Maribelle."

"And what is the 'everyday Maribelle?'" Art asked. "What do you do when you're not here?"

"Not college, that's for sure. I'm skipping that. I'll earn a living here by living frugally, investing my money, and working up to a managerial position," Maribelle replied. "College is a farce. Despite what people say, you don't need it to lead a good life. You just have to be smart enough."

"And you're saying you're smart enough?" Gus asked. She smirked and turned to leave.

"I like to think so." She walked to another table, where she conversed with the young men cheerfully. As the guys watched, she repeated the routine with every table she visited.

"She's, uh, interesting," Neil said. "Flirtatious, cynical, but not necessarily wrong."

"Anyway, back to our previous conversation," Art said, "I've been thinking the same thing as Mikey. I've been dealing with his crap for years. And I think my brothers have as well, especially since hitting high school."

"What would you talk about?" Gus asked.

"It's really frustrating that he expects me to do all these things that I've never wanted to do. He wants me to spend my time reading, studying, and getting a higher education. While these are good things, I also want to play video games and stuff. But he doesn't want what I want, he wants what he and my grandparents want. His head is stuck in his generation and culture, and he's ignoring mine. He's trying to turn me into be the man that he and his parents want me to be, not the man I want to be."

"So tell him that," Mikey said. "Let him know that he's putting too much pressure on you and your brothers. Ask him to let off a bit."

"That and help him understand that you are way different from him," Neil added. "You're growing up in a world completely different from the one of his youth. You're growing up in a culture that defines success as being social and having friends, not making a lot of money and having a high academic degree."

"Yea, America in the twenty-first century is so different from twentieth-century China. We're more into being flashy and outgoing, not studying and learning. Well, most of us." Gus laughed and shrugged. "Hey look, our food!"

Maribelle returned carrying a tray. She set a plate in front of each of the guys. A mound of food sat on top of each plate, consisting of a slice of Texas toast, meat, and a pile of fries. Liquid cheese covered all of this. She picked up their empty glasses and came back with full ones a moment later.

"My body is so ready!" Neil exclaimed, rubbing his hands excitedly.

"Well Mikey, this is it: our first horseshoes as real-ish adults." Gus picked up his fork and scooped cheesy fries into his mouth. "Let's eat!"

"You guys make good points," Art mumbled through a full mouth. "I guess I'll have to talk to my dad soon. Let him know that I want him to stop pushing me to be successful like him. And like with Mikey, I think I need to get all this angst and emotion out in the open to move forward healthily. Writing a paper about it is good, but actually doing it is a totally different thing."

"Do it, man!" Mikey replied. "Explain how you define success for yourself. Maybe even agree to meet in the middle: you can be more studious, and he lower the pressure. We could stop by your house tomorrow or the next day, since we're pretty close."

"Maybe." Art stuffed a huge bite of cheesy fries into his mouth and stopped talking.

"What if we backtrack to Chicago so both of you can talk to your dads?" Neil asked. "It would give us something to do this week before setting off for more sights."

"That could be interesting," Mikey agreed. "But what about you and Gus?"

Gus glanced at Neil and swallowed the food in his mouth. "There's no guarantee to finding Brock. But if you guys want, we can try. There's a lot that we could discuss. It could either be a really short or a really long talk. I would have to creep on his Facebook or try calling my grandparents to find where he lives or works."

"There's nothing for me to do, though," Neil added. "I could visit Dad's grave, but I can't talk to him. I suppose I could try talking to my brother or my mom. And I haven't visited Dad's grave in a couple of years, so I should probably do that if we stop by West Lafayette again."

"Well it's not a matter of us wanting to do it," Mikey replied. "If you don't want to do it, don't. But I think Art and I are both in."

"To be honest," Gus began, "I think we all need this. We've spent so much time ignoring this stuff and running from it. We need to try something different. Close this bad dad chapter once and for all."

"So who's going first?" Art asked. The group exchanged looks before simultaneously turning to look at him. Art sighed and shook his head.

"Your place is the closest," Mikey said. "We can backtrack our route. I'll go next, then Neil, and then Gus will be last. This can be our plan for the week. Then we can figure out what to do after Gus's turn."

"This week, huh?" Gus mused. "Brock's birthday is Friday. That would be one heck of a coincidence! And starting this part of the trip on Father's Day is poetic."

"Fine, I'll go first," Art muttered, stuffing the last bit of his horseshoe into his mouth. "But you guys can't come. You can go to the park down the road, but I'll go inside alone. I don't need you guys awkwardly sitting there while I'm talking to my dad."

"That's fine," Mikey agreed. "I'll probably talk to mine alone too. Neil and Gus can do whatever they want. I'm not going to decide for you. Let us know what you want, and we'll do it."

"That works for me. We'll finish up here and grab a motel," Gus agreed. "Then we can hit the road tomorrow and head for Art's house."

Without another word, they finished their horseshoes and emptied their glasses. Neil got the check from Maribelle and paid for their food.

Loading into the SUV, they found the nearest motel and rented a room for the night.

Art woke up first the next morning. He had
showered and stepped outside by the time Gus
and Mikey woke up. They cleaned themselves up,
and Gus went to find Art as Mikey woke up Neil.

"You're up early. How are you doing, bud?"
Gus joined Art on a bench in the parking lot.

"I'm trying to figure out what to say to Dad,"
he grumbled. "He and I never really talk, so this
will be weird. And there's no way for me to know
how the talk will go. So it's a little nerve-racking
to think about. Plus my blood sugar is all out of
whack because of stress and emotions, and it's
only going to get crazier."

"Yea, this week is going to suck for all of us,"
Gus agreed. "But we should be better off after it.
We'll get to vent all our frustrations to our fathers,
and maybe you and your father will get along better after your talk. Which would make life so
much easier. But regarding your blood sugar,
we'll keep an eye on it, you know that."

"True. Unfortunately we won't know until we
try. And everything is going to suck until then."
Standing up, Art threw his hands up and yelled,

"All right, let's get this over with! Time to chug some Dew and confront my dad!"

Laughing, Gus and Art returned to the motel room to pack their suitcases. Loading up the car, Art switched seats with Gus to ride shotgun and guide Mikey to his house. They pulled some Lunchables from their stock of snacks and ate while on the road.

About half an hour later, they entered Art's hometown, a small town in central Illinois. They passed a Casey's General Store, which according to Art was the town's biggest attraction. He directed them from the main street through a series of turns and side streets until they stopped in front of a two-story white house.

"This is it," Art said solemnly. "If you keep going straight, you'll run into a small park. You guys can hang out there. I'll walk down there and meet you when I'm done." He stepped out of the car and walked up to the front step. Mikey pulled away from the curb as Art opened the door and entered his house.

27

"Travis, is that you?" his mom yelled.

"Yea, it's me!" Art slid off his shoes and left them on the square rug in the foyer. "Is Dad home? I'd like to talk to him."

Footsteps approached from the back of the house. His mother, a petite American woman, met him in the living room. Art's brothers Sean and Vincent were in the living room, reading books and typing on their laptops.

"He's up in his office working," she answered. "What do you need?"

"I need to talk to Dad," Art repeated, climbing the stairs. He walked down the hallway, past the family's bedrooms and toward the office at the back of the house. The door was shut, but he could hear soft instrumental music and the clacking of a keyboard through the door.

Knocking on the door, he opened it and stepped inside. His dad was a small Chinese man with short black hair and glasses. As a lawyer, he always wore a suit, though he loosened his tie and abandoned his jacket and shoes at home.

"Travis, what have I told you about interrupting me while I am working?"

"I need to talk to you, and, um, it can't wait."

"Okay, give me a second." Art's dad typed for a few more moments before stopping and turning around in his chair. "What is wrong?"

"Um, I don't know how else to say this," Art began, "so I'm going to come right out and say it. You, um, you're kind of a crappy father."

"What makes you say that?" Zander asked.

"Well for starters, you show absolutely no emotion! It's ridiculous. You're just a person who lives in my house and tells me how to live my life. There's no emotional connection at all. It's like I'm living with an incredibly bossy rock dressed as a person! Like right now, I said you're a crappy dad, and you didn't react at all."

"I see no point in getting worked up over a simple discussion," he replied calmly. "I show plenty of emotion. I am smiling in every photo we have taken as a family." He gestured around the room, where various family pictures hung.

"That's not the same! The only emotion I've ever felt from you is disappointment. You were never proud of what I did, never happy with the effort I put into anything. All you ever showed was disappointment! In my studies, in my hobbies, in my friends, in my girlfriends, in anything and everything that took my attention!"

"I wanted you to do your best, Travis. I was top of my class in secondary school. I spent all of my time studying and reading. The only friends I had were people who would help me to get into the best universities and give the best references for my résumé. As for girlfriends, I never dated until I moved to America. There was nothing to distract me from my studies: no movies, video games, parties, or anything. Back home, nobody wanted to do any of that. We have been taught for generations that we need to do well in school so that we could become successful and respected working men and women."

"But we're not in China!" Art snapped. "This is America! Kids play video games, go to movies, sneak out, and throw parties! There's enough time in the day for me to do those things and still get my school work done!"

"Your brothers do not do any of those things," his father replied. "They are very studious. Sean was top of his class, and he is excelling at Harvard. Vincent is second in his class, but he is going to Princeton in the fall to study engineering. Both of them are going to be very successful.

"But I wanted you to be more like them. You had the potential to be the top of your class and wasted it. And you could be an honors student now, but instead you barely avoid flunking out of college. You are my eldest son, so you should carry on the family name with honor. You need to be successful in order to do that."

"I didn't want to be like them! I didn't want to be the top of my class, and I don't want to be an honors student! I want to have fun while at college! I want you and Mom to support me and to be proud of me, not of my grades or my popularity! I want you to see that I'm not you, that I'm growing up and maturing even if it is differently than you did! I want you to let me be myself."

"I am proud of you. I simply think that—"

"No!" Art yelled. "Just be proud of me! I'll graduate from college next year! I'm going to be a counselor so that I can help people! I have great friends who encourage me to do my best and to be myself! You have this image of me that's basically a mini version of you! I understand that Grandma and Grandpa raised you a certain way, but that way doesn't work for me! I don't want to be the best. I just want to be myself, and I want you and Mom to acknowledge that! I don't mean to dishonor you or Mom. I want to honor you by living the life that I want."

Art's dad sat silent for several moments, staring blankly into the corner. Art caught his breath as either tears or more yelling bubbling just under the surface. He suddenly realized that all energy was gone from his body. As he pulled out his meter to check his blood sugar, Zander handed him a Pepsi from the mini-fridge beside his desk.

"Let me get this straight," his dad said. "You think I am pushing you too hard to become something that you do not want to be. Correct?"

"Yea," Art grumbled, sipping on the Pepsi. "I don't want to become a doctor or study and work all day. I want to help people. And I want to play video games, go out with friends, and stay up too late. I want to get married and have kids and be the most fun, most involved dad ever."

"Is that how you define success?"

"Yes. If I can do all that, I will be successful. And I'll be me."

His dad paused again. Then he stood up, walked over to Art, and placed his hands on his son's shoulders. "I do not know if Grandma and Grandpa will understand, but I think I do. I am proud of you, Travis. You have grown into quite the young man. You proved that just now by saying what you needed to say, knowing that I might not understand. Thank you for that. I am glad that you know what success means to you, even if it is different from my definition."

Art his dad in the eyes before wrapping his arms around him in a hug. He could not fight the tears anymore.

"I did learn a lot from you. I learned to appreciate education. I may not be the best student, but I'm really good at reading and studying. If I put the time and effort into something, I can do really well at it."

"Then why is it that your grades are so low?" his dad asked, smirking.

"I'm just lazy," Art admitted. "Being a good friend is more important to me."

"Ah, I see. Well I am glad that you have found some good friends and that you are doing what brings you joy. I am proud of you."

"Thanks Dad," was all he could say.

"You are welcome son."

28

After Art opened the front door, Mikey drove down the road and found the park. He parked the car and led Gus and Neil to the swing set. Not knowing how long Art would be at his house, they sat on the swings and waited.

Neil started swinging after a few minutes. He swung his legs and kicked off the ground to swing higher. "While we're waiting, we might as well have fun!" he said loudly. "Let's see who can jump the farthest!"

"What is this, elementary school?" Gus taunted as he started to swing. Mikey followed their lead, and soon all three were taking turns jumping off the swings.

Gus and Mikey consistently fought for first place, with Mikey ultimately winning when they stopped. As he gloated over his victory, he noticed a roundabout on the other side of the park.

"Dude!" he yelled, pointing. "I haven't been on one of those in years!"

"Let's go!" Neil agreed. "Most playgrounds and parks don't have them anymore!" They ran over to the roundabout and climbed on.

The three took turns spinning their friends. The roundabout squeaked and groaned the entire time. Occasionally, one of the guys would lose his grip on the rails and tumbled into the grass, laughing and yelling.

"Hey guys." Art had approached them without any of their notice, carrying a plastic bag. "I see you're enjoying the park. I don't think I've seen anyone play here in years. And certainly not anyone older than like seven."

"Oh hey Art!" Gus greeted, standing up. The guys found a nearby bench and sat down to talk about what happened.

"So how did the talk with your dad go?" Mikey asked.

Art recounted the conversation between him and his dad. His friends remained silent the entire time. "And after we talked, we went downstairs for dinner. Mom made General Tso's chicken with white rice and vegetables."

"Dude!" Neil exclaimed. "I want some General Tso's!"

"That's what's in here," Art answered, holding up the bag. "I have a giant Tupperware container of leftovers. We can heat it up after we find a motel for the night."

"Sounds like a plan!" Neil agreed.

"But, uh, while we were eating, we talked about how school was going," Art continued. "My parents wanted to clarify their expectations of me, so we talked about all of that. They wanted to know how to encourage me along the way, and I told them what I thought of their expectations. When they were too high, we discussed how to lower them to be realistic."

"That's good," Gus noted. "Do you think the talk went well?"

"Yea, I do." Art paused. "Dad said that he wanted me to be like my brothers, because they both are studious and successful like him. But I think he realized that I'm different from them, which is important. And he seemed to approve of my view success."

"That's awesome!" Mikey cheered. "You should text him and wish him a happy Father's Day, even though it's a day late."

"Good idea," Art agreed. "I'll do that when we get to a motel. In fact, I'll call him. Let's go!"

Art traded high fives with his friends, who patted him on the back as they walked to the car.

Mikey's phone guided them to the nearest motel, which was about half an hour away. Renting a room, they settled in and heated up the leftover Chinese food. They found a movie on Netflix and started eating as Art pulled out his phone and left the room.

"Mikey, dude, it's time to wake up!" Gus shook his friend until he opened his eyes.

"What time is it?" he grumbled, covering his eyes with his arm.

"It's 1 o'clock," Neil answered. He and Art sat on the other bed in their room. They had already loaded their suitcases into Mikey's SUV to leave.

"Oh gosh. Why didn't you wake me up?" Mikey stood up and rubbed his eyes. He stumbled to the bathroom.

"Well we figured you were tired after all the driving you've done lately," Gus said. "Since we're not in any hurry, we just let you sleep. Plus, what does it look like we're doing, stupid?"

"Plus it's your turn to talk to your dad," Art added. "I wasn't too excited to talk to mine, so I bet you aren't either. Now we have all afternoon to drive back up north before you talk to him tonight or tomorrow."

The room was silent except for running water in the bathroom. Mikey emerged a few minutes later with his toiletries. He combed his hair and changed clothes before packing his suitcase and loading it into his vehicle.

"All right," he said, coming back into the room. "Let's check out and hit the road."

"So what's the plan?" Gus asked as they pulled onto the interstate. He shifted in the passenger seat to face Mikey. Neil watched over Art's shoulder as he played on his Vita, mumbling about the game.

"Well, I'm not sure," Mikey began. "I don't know whether my dad will be at work tonight. We could probably crash in the attic, where I normally stay. My sisters have the basement, and my youngest siblings have the upstairs bedrooms."

"Okay. So are we just going to go to your place and work from there?"

Mikey paused. "Yea, we can do that. You guys can watch Netflix or something in the attic while I talk to my dad. Though if he's not home, chances are that we'll have to babysit my siblings. You may even get to see Jenny and Suzie, since it's summertime."

"You know, we've never actually met your sisters," Neil interrupted. "You just talk about them all the time!"

"Do you not remember graduation? They were totally there, dummy." Mikey chuckled. "Though if they are home, they'll probably ditch us immediately to hang out with their friends. Leave us to babysit."

"Oh well," Gus replied. "Have you decided what to say? Did you write your letter?"

"Probably swear at him and punch him in the face," Mikey said seriously. "Kidding, I'll avoid those as much as possible. The letter talks about all the ways that he was a good dad to me. I focused on the good, but I may not be that level-headed in person. Regardless of what happens, I'll give him the letter before we leave."

"How do you think he'll respond?" Art asked. "We had similar experiences with our dads, but yours is still a different person from mine."

Mikey sighed heavily before responding. "I really don't know what he'll say. He can be unpredictable and hard-headed."

"So that's where you get it," Gus interrupted, sticking out his tongue.

"Shut up!" Mikey punched him. "Anyway, I can see it going any number of ways. Based on past conversations though, I think it will take a lot of convincing for him to realize where he went wrong. He'll do everything to justify his actions. But maybe reading the letter will do something that talking to him can't do."

"I can see that," Gus agreed, rubbing his shoulder. "You've told me plenty of stories, so I have a pretty good idea of how you two relate. I would say you're right. He seems set in his ways, so expect the worst."

"I'll try, but you never know what will happen." Mikey fell silent, and they continued along the interstate in silence. The only noise in the SUV came from Art's Vita and Neil's commentary on the game.

"I think we need some tunes," Neil said after a few minutes. "I have Spotify Premium, so hook me up and I'll DJ." Gus turned on the Bluetooth, and Neil connected his phone to the radio.

"Make sure you play something good!" Mikey demanded.

"I think I have the perfect song to play." Neil smirked as music started playing.

"'The Great Escape!' Boys Like Girls!" Mikey cheered, laughing. As the song picked up, the guys rolled down their windows and jammed out. They sang loudly, pumped their fists out the window, and danced around in their seats. All the cars passing them on the interstate shot perplexed looks at them.

As the song ended, they busted out laughing. Gus turned down the radio as Mikey rolled up their windows.

"Funny story about that song," Neil added. "It's basically a graduation song. The song writer described it as the end of one chapter with an outlook on the future."

"Huh," Mikey mumbled. "That's oddly perfect for us. Good job, Spotify."

"Um, excuse you, I picked the song. I'll take that credit."

"My bad. Good job, Spotify Premium." Mikey winked at Neil in the rearview.

Neil continued to play upbeat songs as they continued north. When a favorite song started, they jammed out to it as they did with 'The Great Escape.' Before long, Mikey exited from the interstate and headed for Rockford, his hometown.

"Do you actually live in Rockford?" Art asked. "I don't think any of us have been up here to visit your home."

"I live on the outskirts of town," Mikey answered. "In town is a tad too crazy for us. We should be there soon."

When they arrived at Mikey's house, they pulled into a long driveway leading to a large blue house. A tall wooden fence enclosed the backyard, and Gus noticed an expansive garden along the side of the house. A garage sat a short distance from the house, with three cars sitting in front of it.

"The SUV is Mom's," Mikey explained. "The Jeep is Jenny's, and I think the Ford is Suzie's. Dad drives a big truck, so I guess he's still at work." As they parked, Mikey's sisters stepped onto the front porch to see who was here.

"Oh hey, it's Mike!" one of them shouted. Jenny had her short brown hair pulled back and wore basketball shorts with a band shirt.

"Hey Jenny," Mikey said, walking up to the porch. Gus followed him, while Art and Neil got out of the car. "You remember the guys, right?"

"Long time no see!" Jenny smiled broadly and shook Gus's hand.

"I remember you now!" Neil exclaimed.

"Did you forget that you met us like a month ago?" Suzie asked. "Lame. Anyway, the house is a bit of a mess. And I have to unpack and organize my room." Suzie turned and walked back into the house.

Jenny and the guys followed her into the house. They kicked off their shoes in the foyer and entered the living room, where Michelle was watching the news in her scrubs.

"Hey Mike, hey boys!" She stood up and hugged them. "What brings you here?"

"I wanted to talk to Dad," Mikey replied. "Is he still at work?"

"Yea, he'll be home late tonight. What did you want to talk to him about?" Mikey's mom went into the kitchen and started preparing dinner. "Also, are you guys going to be around for dinner? We're having spaghetti!"

"I wanted to talk to him one-on-one," Mikey said. "Yea, we'll be here for dinner. Is it fine if we stay here tonight? We'll sleep in my room."

"That's fine," she answered. "I'll let you all know when dinner is ready, so you can go ahead and settle in for the night."

Mikey showed the guys around the house quickly. Downstairs, the front door opened to the kitchen, which led into the living room. At the back of the house, Mikey showed them the dining room and the master bedroom. Upstairs, they found three bedrooms, two bathrooms, and a staircase to the attic.

The guys retrieved their suitcases and headed to the attic. The attic was a large room, with piles of boxes in the corner. A queen-sized bed sat against the far wall, by the only window in the room. A couch and lounge chair sat in front of a large flat-screen TV in the middle of the room.

"Dibs on the bed!" Neil declared, hurrying across the room.

"I mean, it's my bed, so you'll have to share," Mikey said. He turned to Art and Gus. "One of you can take the couch, and the other can take the chair or the floor."

"I'll sleep on the floor," Gus volunteered. "What are we going to do?"

"We can watch more Netflix or play video games," Mikey suggested. "Or we can grab a board game from the living room."

"Let's play a board game," Neil replied. "We haven't done that yet." He and Mikey went downstairs to grab a board game, while Art and Gus settled in. They pushed the couch back to make more room around the coffee table.

"We have Monopoly and Life," Neil said, coming back into the room.

"Do you have any cards?" Art asked. "I could teach you to play Cheat or Egyptian."

"That sounds fun! We should have a couple decks somewhere."

Mikey dug through boxes and finally found a deck of cards. They sat on the floor and started playing Cheat. By the time they finished, Mikey's mom yelled that dinner was ready. They joined her, Jenny, and Suzie at the table. A smaller table sat nearby, where the younger siblings ate.

Jenny shared some of her social work practicum experiences, while Suzie talked about her political science studies. Michelle shared embarrassing stories from Mikey's childhood, while Neil and Art told stories from college.

After dinner, they returned to the attic to play Egyptian, turning on some background music. The first game progressed slowly as Art taught his friends. But soon they were throwing cards, slapping the table, and shouting nonstop. Later they heard a car pull into the drive.

Mikey went to the window and glanced out. "That's Dad," he muttered. "Be right back." He sighed and headed downstairs.

29

"Hey Dad," Mikey said, stepping into the garage. Randy leaned over his workbench with a beer in his hand.

"Hey Michael. How's your road trip going?"

"It's been fun." Mikey stood in the middle of the garage, not wanting to sit or approach his dad. "I've enjoyed spending time with the guys. We've had a lot of fun and seen a lot of different places lately."

"That's good," his dad muttered. "Do you want to sit? There are beers in the fridge." He pulled a stool from under his bench and gestured toward the fridge in the corner.

"No, I'm fine." Mikey sighed heavily. "Dad, I need to talk to you."

"What's up?" The man turned around and leaned back against the workbench.

"Well, I wanted to come clean about some things that I should've said sooner. I, um, don't really know how to say this well, so I'll just say it. I pretty much hated my childhood. I didn't really have a childhood, because I spent all of my time working to pay for everything and babysitting the kids. It wasn't fair."

"Fair?" his dad grumbled. "I worked on your grandparents' farm from the time I could walk. Grandpa would wake me up at the crack of dawn to milk the cows and gather the eggs. I was baling hay and driving the tractor from the age of ten. I simply raised you the way I was raised: to be responsible and hard-working."

"I am both of those things! I've paid for my phone and car since I was fifteen! Then I worked a full-time job while taking classes full-time at college. I did my best at everything I did, and I've never needed any financial help from you! You've even had me working my ass off to raise your children since I was ten years old!"

"See, I made you the man you are today. You could never have done any of that if not for me instilling those values in you from youth."

"Yea, you made me responsible and hard-working, but that's not all I am! Do you even realize all the crap I went through because of you? You've forced me to do what *you* wanted my entire life! You only allowed me to date girls you chose, and then you forced me to study education at college! You never let me do what I wanted! Now I'm all screwed up because I don't know what I want out of life. For the first time, I can make my own decisions, but I don't know what to do! All because you made every decision for me my entire life!"

"Michael, you need to understand something." His dad walked to the fridge to grab another beer. He offered one to Mikey again, who declined. "You are the oldest child and my son. You should be the most responsible and mature one. So I raised you that way. But with your sisters, I raised them much differently because they aren't the oldest and they aren't boys. I still encourage them to work hard and become responsible, but I don't force them to do that. That's your mother's responsibility."

"But what parents leave their ten-year-old son to babysit every weekend?" Mikey was nearly yelling at this point. "Kids want to play and have fun, not be the parent to their siblings!"

"Grandpa did the same to me, and it taught me responsibility. I was trying to do the same for you," his dad replied. "Every child needs to understand that their actions affect others. I wanted you to learn to think about the needs of others aside from yourself. That is why your mother and I let you babysit your siblings."

"But I didn't need you to be just like Grandpa! I needed you to be better. That's a dad's job, right, to be better to his kids than his dad was to him? But you weren't!" Mikey paused to take a deep breath. "You did what was easiest for you, not caring how it affected me. All to teach me 'responsibility!' You left me to raise myself and made yourself feel better by telling yourself that it worked for you! And that's not fair!"

Mikey's dad sighed and rubbed his eyes, exasperated. "You're too young to see what I was doing. I'm sorry you don't understand yet." He stood up and walked toward Mikey.

Mikey felt his blood boiling. When his dad moved to pass him, he grabbed the collar of his shirt and pulled him so that they were face-to-face. He started speaking through gritted teeth.

"You're sorry that I don't understand? I understand! I understand that you're a dick. You're a horrible father! I understand that you have no idea who I am or what I want because you're stuck on your high horse thinking that you've done no wrong! And I understand that you really aren't sorry! You wouldn't change a thing about how you raised me!" He breathed heavily as his father shook his head.

Suddenly, Randy shoved his son away from him. Mikey stumbled backward into the shelves behind him. He glared at his father, who had turned and continued out the door. He paused in the doorway.

"Clearly I didn't raise you as well as Grandpa raised me," he said without turning around. He walked away, leaving Mikey alone in the garage.

Walking out of the garage, he pulled out his phone and dialed Amber's number. He started wandering the property as the phone rang.

"Hey love," she greeted. "What's up?"

"I talked to my dad," he replied gruffly. He quickly told her about their conversation.

"Wow, that sucks," Amber said. "How are you feeling?"

"To be honest, like I want to beat the tar out of my dad. Like I want to yell and scream and hit him until he understands how screwed up I am because of him. That's all. I just want him to understand."

"I know you do. But sometimes people are too stubborn and set in their ways. They've convinced themselves that they're correct for so long that being wrong isn't something they can even consider. He's been telling himself that he raised you the right way for twenty-two years now. Being wrong isn't an option for him."

"That doesn't make it hurt any less," Mikey mumbled, tears welling up. "It still sucks! It hurts so much. I just want it to stop. I want him to say he's sorry, to admit that he's wrong and that he hurt me."

"But he did the best he could," she reassured him. "You heard how he was raised. He had to work and be responsible from a young age. That's all he knew. He didn't know any other way to raise you. I think that counts for something, even if it is only an explanation."

Mikey remained silent for a moment, thinking about her words. "I guess you're right. He did what he thought was best for me. But that doesn't excuse it. He still left me broken and hurting, and I don't think those wounds will ever fully heal."

"Maybe they won't. But they don't have to cripple you. Sometimes the deepest, most painful wounds can motivate you to overcome, to become better than those who hurt you. So pick yourself up, nurse your wounds, and become a better man, husband, and father than your dad ever was. Oh, and you might want to start by apologizing for your last comments. You might have crossed a line there."

Sighing, Mikey responded, "You're right. I was thinking the same thing. I'll apologize if I see him before we leave, and if not, I'll call him later. I do still have the letter to give to him."

"Good. Are you feeling better?" Amber asked.

"Yea, I am. I better get back upstairs to the guys. Talk to you soon!" Mikey hung up the phone and headed toward the house.

30

"This game is so intense," Gus said as they continued playing Egyptian. "I might have a heart attack. I'm pretty sure I've been having an adrenaline rush for half an hour now."

"Seriously," Neil agreed. "I can hardly think about anything other than — Art! Dang it! Those cards should be mine!"

"Well maybe you should get good, scrub!" he teased, picking up the stack of cards in the middle. "While you two are busy flapping your jaws, I'll just win another round."

"Maybe we should play something else after this," Gus suggested.

"*Call of Duty*!" Art exclaimed, slapping the pile of cards and picking them up.

"Yea! You suck at that!" Neil teased. "We would totally destroy you!"

Gus shrugged, so they started *Call of Duty* on the PlayStation. They played a free-for-all game, so they started sneaking around the map to shoot each other. Gus was the first to die, falling before he could even find whomever was shooting him.

"How do you think Mikey's talk with his dad is going?" Neil asked suddenly.

"Probably about as well as we can expect," Art replied. "We've all heard his stories about how poorly they get along."

"Yea, I doubt it's going as well as Art's conversation did," Gus added. "How long has it been since he left?"

Neil picked up his phone. "Umm, half an hour. So he should be back soon."

As gameplay continued, they fell silent apart from yelling in response to getting shot and killed. Gus managed a few kills, but his friends killed him more than he killed them. Before long, they heard footsteps on the stairs and paused the game as Mikey entered the room. He stopped inside the doorway and stared at the floor.

An awkward silence filled the room before Art spoke up. "How did it go?"

Mikey walked over to them and sat down on the coffee table. He related how the talk went with his dad and what Amber had said when he called her. As he finished, he walked to the fridge and grabbed them bottles of Dr. Pepper.

"Well it sounds like it went better than expected!" Neil joked. Mikey dropped a bottle and kicked it aggressively at him, shaking the soda.

"What are you going to do now?" Art asked. "Like, right now and after we finish our road trip. Do you have any plans?"

"Right now, I'm going to unwind with some video games. As for after the road trip, I'll figure that out." Mikey grabbed a controller and joined Gus and Art on the couch. "I'll be fine. I just need to get my mind off things for now. Who's up for some *Worms*?"

The next morning, Gus awoke to someone shaking his shoulder. Opening his eyes, he saw a blurry Mikey kneeling right next to him on the floor. He could hear Art snoring, so he assumed that Neil was also still asleep.

"Dude, let's go make some breakfast," Mikey suggested. "It's about 9 o'clock. We can make something home-cooked and wake these bozos up to eat."

"Okay," Gus croaked, groggy. "I'll meet you downstairs in half an hour." As Mikey went downstairs, Gus showered and got dressed. Then he headed down to the kitchen.

Walking into the room, Gus saw food cluttering the countertops. Mikey had pulled cartons of eggs, a couple pounds of bacon, tubes of cinnamon rolls, and a bag of frozen hash browns from the fridge. Gus found him sitting on the counter eating a bowl of cereal.

"Let's do this," he said, putting his bowl in the sink. "We can probably cook the eggs, bacon, and hash browns at the same time. Which do you want to do?"

"Well first, we should start the cinnamon rolls. Those will take a while." Gus paused to consider his options. "I'll do the bacon and eggs. I can keep the bacon chewy, which is how I prefer it, but I'll make most of it crunchy. You can find some pancake mix and make some pancakes. Or preferably waffles, if you have a waffle maker."

"I have one packed away in my room. Do we want plain waffles or something fancy? Chocolate chip, fruit, peanut butter?"

"Definitely chocolate chip," Gus answered, cracking eggs into a bowl.

"Perfect!" They immediately got to work frying the bacon and hash browns, scrambling the eggs, and baking the cinnamon rolls. Gus frequently yelped in pain and jerked his arms away from the stovetop as the bacon grease popped and splattered him, which Mikey found funny. Mikey ran upstairs after mixing some batter and returned with the waffle maker.

Within half an hour, they had set the dining room table. They placed bowls full of eggs, bacon, and hash browns in the middle, surrounding plates of cinnamon rolls and waffles. Gus poured glasses of chocolate milk and apple juice for the four of them. As Mikey returned to the attic to wake up their friends, Gus pulled a bag of shredded cheese from the fridge for Neil.

The next hour was full of talking, laughter, and the clattering of dishes and silverware. When they finished, Art and Neil cleaned the dining room and kitchen while their friends packed their suitcases and carried them to the SUV. By noon, the guys piled into the car to head to West Lafayette, with Neil riding shotgun.

31

"What haven't we eaten?" Mikey asked as they neared Lafayette. "Something good."

"I mean, we can always go back to Triple XXX," Neil said. Then he muttered quickly, "Maybe Crystal is working tonight."

"Are you gonna try to get her number?" Art teased. Neil snatched the phone from his hand, and Art punched him in retaliation. "What about B Dubs? We haven't had wings yet!"

"Oh yes!" Mikey shouted excitedly. He reached into the backseat and patted Gus on the knee. "You owe us B Dubs, dude."

"Oh he does? Why?" Neil turned suddenly in his seat and stared at Gus, grinning.

Gus chuckled and shook his head. "It's true. We raced to our cars and wagered B Dubs. We didn't know who won, so I volunteered to buy, and he Manchestered me."

"Well I guess we need to go to B Dubs!" Neil looked expectantly at Mikey.

"All right, to B Dubs!" he announced. He then glanced in his rearview mirror and winked at Gus. "And if you don't pay, I'll slap you so hard that it'll make your head spin!"

"Don't worry, I'll pay," Gus assured. "I mean, I get B Dubs out of the deal!"

"And for once, I don't have to pay!" Neil added, turning up the radio.

Mikey accelerated down the interstate. As they crossed the state line, Neil rolled his window down, stuck his head out, and hollered into the wind. The others joined him in yelling but remained in the vehicle.

At Buffalo Wild Wings, they each ordered Mountain Dew and a large servings of honey barbecue and Asian zing wings, with Gus adding a large order of fries. The televisions around them played an array of sports.

"Is there rugby?" Neil asked, looking around. "I love rugby! It's so intense."

"Seriously," Gus agreed. "I don't like sports, but I still respect rugby players. Plus all of them are totally jacked!"

"What do you do at B Dubs, since you don't watch sports?" Mikey watched the various soccer games happening above their heads. Meanwhile, Art checked his blood sugar.

"I usually stick with UFC, track and field, and the quiz game," Gus answered. "I never actually play the quiz, but I try to see how well I would do against those who are playing."

"You like UFC?" Neil asked. "I know you ran track in high school, so that makes sense. But I didn't expect you to like UFC."

"Well I wrestled in high school, and it's kind of similar to wrestling. Plus, it's always fun to see two guys beat the tar out of each other. And it's an added bonus when someone takes a jab to the head and immediately crumples to the ground."

When their food arrived, the guy turned their attention from the screens to their wings. Conversation died at the table as they began devouring their food. Their waiter disappeared until they were nearly done, when they waved him down to request take-home boxes.

"That was so good!" Gus exclaimed, sitting back in his seat.

"I mean, it's B Dubs," Art replied. "What else do you expect?"

"Absolutely nothing," Neil said. "And now we'll have leftovers to eat later tonight!"

"That's the best way to eat wings," Mikey answered. "It's a little expensive for a single meal. Speaking of expensive, don't forget to pay, Gus!"

"I won't," he assured them. "In the meantime, why don't you guys figure out where we're staying tonight?"

"Oh that's easy," Neil interrupted. "Some of my buddies have a bachelor pad on the other side of town. I hang out there all the time."

"Are they okay with all of us crashing there?" Gus handed his debit card to the waiter when he returned with the boxes.

"Oh yea, I already asked them." Neil laughed and dumped his wings into his box. "They left on vacation last weekend and won't be back until next week. I already have a key, so it's fine."

"Sweet, let's roll then! I'll cover the tip." Mikey dropped some cash on the table as the waiter returned with Gus's card. Signing the receipt, he joined his friends outside. They took their seats in Mikey's SUV and followed Neil's directions across town.

"Here it is," Neil said, pointing at a small white house. It was a single-story building with an attached one-car garage. A basketball hoop hung above the garage door. Neil unlocked the door and led them inside.

The front door opened into the living room, which had two leather couches and a large flat-screen TV mounted on the wall. A stretch of countertop divided this room from the kitchen, with bar stools lined on the living room side. In the corner of the kitchen, Gus noticed a door that he assumed led to the garage. At the back of the house, Neil showed them three small bedrooms and the bathroom.

"Make yourselves at home! There are plenty of snacks and drinks in the kitchen. We have plenty of movies to watch and video games to play. Or we could go to the garage and play ping-pong or pool."

"I'm down for some pool," Mikey replied. "We can play 2-v-2."

"I'm on Mikey's team," Gus declared. "We'll destroy you guys!" They headed through the kitchen into the garage. A pool table sat in the middle of the room, with a ping-pong table nearby. A large fridge stood in the corner, and several tall bar tables littered the room.

"Let's turn on some tunes." Neil connected his phone to a sound system that was hidden in a wardrobe next to the fridge. Music began playing from the speakers surrounding the room while Mikey racked the pool balls.

They played pool for the rest of the night. They would shuffle teams after a couple of games and switch to playing cutthroat. The guys danced, sang, and played air guitar along with the music throughout the night. After a couple of games, they started to discuss their plans for the next day.

"So Neil," Mikey began. "How do you want to go about tomorrow?"

"Well I want to visit Dad's grave," he replied. "We can do that first. I think that's the most important part."

"Okay, sounds good," Mikey agreed.

"What about your brother?" Art asked. "Or your mom? Could you call either of them?"

Neil sighed and remained silent for a moment. "I'm not sure. I don't even know what I would say to either of them. How do you talk about the void left from your dad's death? And how do you tell the people closest to you that you've been faking it for as long as you can remember?"

"Have you written your letter yet?" Mikey asked. "That helped me a lot, and I'm sure it helped Art."

"Yea, but I wrote that like I was talking to Dad one last time. I told him about what he's missed of my life, about what I want to do when I graduate, about you guys, about how I've handled him being gone. It's not a letter to Mom or Matt."

"But that's a start," Art replied. "You've already put those things down on paper. Now you can just bring them up to your mom or brother. You don't even need to talk about what's in the letter. The assignment could just be a segue to talking about your dad."

"Or you don't even need to talk," Gus added. "You can just be with one of them at your dad's grave. If conversation happens, cool. If not, cool. Just as long as you aren't alone."

"Yea, I guess." Neil paused and took a deep breath. "We'll leave when we all get up and moving. Maybe I'll text Matt and see if he can meet us there. If not, I always have you losers."

The conversation died as they returned their focus to the game. Around eleven o'clock, they returned to the living room to start a movie. Mikey grabbed *The Fast and the Furious* from a shelf and started it. Before long, the group had drifted off.

32

They pulled into the cemetery the next afternoon. Neil directed them toward a group of headstones around the middle of the cemetery. Mikey parked the car, and the guys followed Neil to a row of graves. Gus glanced at the names written and noticed that many of them shared Neil's last name: McAvoy.

"These are Dad's relatives," he explained sullenly. "His parents, aunts and uncles, and a handful of cousins. Here's Dad." He stopped in front of a headstone that read, 'Ritchie McAvoy.'

"We'll give you some space, bro," Art said quietly. "If you need us, holler." Neil simply nodded, so his friends returned to the SUV to wait.

Neil stood in front of his father's grave, his mind blank. He had no idea what to think or feel. He felt strangely numb, but the numbness slowly gave way to the weight of sadness. He pulled his letter out of his back pocket and sat down in front of the headstone.

"It sucks, you know," he mumbled, picking at the grass. "I don't know what happened to you after you died, but I know what happened to me. I went through hell. I was just a kid, really. I didn't know how to handle the pain. So I tried to numb it with whatever I could: drugs, alcohol, even girls and sex. But it never left. It's like I have this giant scab on my heart, and sometimes it starts to peel and bleed for seemingly no reason.

"Now here I am, six years later. I made a lot of mistakes in high school, but you weren't here to tell me what to do. I discovered sex and drugs and all of that on my own because you weren't here to teach me about them. I'm going to finish college soon, but you aren't here to shake my hand or say you're proud of me. I have better friends than I could've ever imagined, but you aren't here to meet them. One day, I hope to get married and have kids of my own, but you won't be there to watch me grow up or to spoil your grandkids."

Neil paused and blinked the tears from his eyes. "It sucks. I've had to figure things out on my own. I've struggled pretty much nonstop since you died. People say it gets better, but the pain just doesn't go away."

Neil fell silent for a few moments. He heard a car door shut but thought nothing of it, assuming it was one of his friends grabbing a drink. Suddenly someone rustled his hair aggressively and sat down next to him.

"Sup bro," Matt said. He was heavy-set man of average height, with spiky hair and a skull and crossbones tattoo on his left forearm. He wore faded jeans and a plain black shirt.

"What are you doing here?"

Matt pointed over his shoulder. "Your buddy Mikey texted me this morning. Told me that you'd be here and asked if I wanted to come by. So how are you doing?"

"Eh, you know how it goes. Father's Day."

"I totally understand. I make sure I work or sleep all day so that I don't have to think about it. It doesn't really get much easier, it seems."

"Really?" Neil turned to look at his brother. "How did you do it? How did you handle Dad's death so well? I never saw you cry or anything."

"Just because you didn't see it doesn't mean it didn't happen," Matt replied, chuckling. "I struggled a lot. I had to keep my composure around you and Mom, because you needed someone to keep their head straight. But when I was away from home, I fell into the same things you did:

partying, drinking, and drugs. Some days got so bad that I, uh, took a razor to myself. I...have scars all over my thighs from that. Suddenly I was man of the house, and I had no idea how to handle that kind of responsibility. So I ran from it and pushed it from my mind with anything that would distract me.

"But then I ran into you at a frat party. I saw you hurting just as much as me, if not more. I realized that I had to get my shit together for your sake. So I took you home and decided to stop going to parties and hooking up with chicks. I started taking my role as man of the house seriously. I visited Uncle Jon the next day and broke down. He helped me to keep clean and taught me how to be more responsible. I know I could never replace Dad, but I did the best I could with Uncle Jon's help to make it easier for you and Mom.

"You know, that's why I taught you about computers. It gave us something to do together, which let me talk to you and see how you were coping. Plus you could focus on the computers. It provided something of a normal routine, when everything in your life seemed to fall apart around you. Computers were something Dad taught me, so it seemed right to pass it on to you.

Had he been around longer, he would've done the same."

"Wow, I didn't know that." Neil fell silent for a moment. "Life just sucks for all of us, doesn't it? You and me, and all of those guys."

"Yea, it really does," Matt agreed. "I only talked to Mikey a bit this morning, but he told me a bit about each of their issues with their dads. They understand, bro. They've been fighting the same fight as us. In ways, they've been fighting it longer. Yea, their circumstances are different than ours, but the fight is the same. We're fighting our pasts. And it's always going to be a losing battle when you fight it alone."

"That's true. We've had many talks about how our dads or lives suck. It was so nice to talk about it after thinking I was alone for so long," Neil admitted. "You and Mom never talked about it, so it felt like I was the only one who had no idea what to do. It felt like I was drowning while everyone else was safe and okay on the shore."

"Well that is absolutely not true. Mom and I were drowning with you. And your friends have been struggling to stay afloat all their lives. That's often the life of a fatherless kid: teaching yourself how to live. And look at where you guys are now. Look how far you've come. You beat the odds.

Statistics say that you should be druggies, gang members, or criminals. You should be in prison or dead. But you guys took your pain and used it to become the men you are today."

The pair fell silent for a moment before Neil sighed and handed his letter to Matt. "I wrote this letter not too long ago. It's all the stuff that I wish Dad could be here to do with me. Everything I've done since he died and everything I want to do. There's so much that he's already missed, and it really hurt remembering all of it. But then I started looking ahead, and that hurt even worse. He'll never see me graduate college or marry the woman of my dreams and have kids.

"But as I was wallowing in my self-pity, I realized something. I can't live in the past. I can't linger on wondering what might have been. I have to move on, or else I might as well be dead. Dad is gone, and there's no changing that. Maybe he'd be proud of me, maybe he wouldn't be. But he sure as hell wouldn't be proud of me living that way. If I want him to be proud of me, I have to live life to the fullest. And that's what the end of that letter talks about. I'm going to live, not in spite of Dad's absence but because of it."

"That," Matt said slowly, "is some good wisdom, Neil. I never would've thought to tell you that, so I'm glad that you figured it out for yourself. I guess I realized the same thing, just in a slightly different way. That would explain me cleaning up my act."

Matt paused and stood up. Patting Neil on the shoulder, he said, "Dad would be proud of you, by the way. You've grown into one hell of a young man. So don't let yourself get too down. Remember that you can talk to those guys, and they'll understand. More importantly, never forget that Dad would be proud of you. I know Mom and I are too."

"Thanks Matt. I guess I don't really need that anymore," Neil said, nodding at his letter. "I'll just leave it here. This seems like the perfect place for it."

Neil stood up as Matt tucked the letter into the dirt surrounding the headstone. The pair returned to Neil's friends. They leaned against the side of Mikey's SUV, quietly waiting for Neil. When Neil approached, Art was the first to say anything.

"How was it?" he asked.

"Not too bad," Neil replied. "It could've been worse. Matt and I had a good talk. I'll fill you guys in later."

"I have to go, bro," Matt said. "I work in a couple of hours. It was good talking to you! And Mikey, thanks for texting me." He hugged Neil, patted Mikey on the shoulder, and left.

"Oh yea, that reminds me!" Neil shoved Mikey. "You stole my brother's number from my phone, didn't you? There's no other way for you to get it!"

Mikey laughed and shoved him back. "I'm not apologizing. Let's head back to the pad and figure out what we're doing next." Piling into the SUV, they left the cemetery and returned to the bachelor pad.

33

"Your turn now, Gus," Neil said, taking a seat at the counter. Art and Mikey joined him while Gus grabbed cans of Mountain Dew from the fridge before sitting down.

"Yea, I know. I'm, uh, I'm not super excited about that."

"What's the plan, bro?" Mikey asked. "We should figure out where we're going and what we're doing before we go anywhere. Do you know where Brock lives or works?"

"Last I knew, he lived in a trailer on a random backroad near Crawfordsville," Gus replied. "Though I know his wife lived in Crawfordsville somewhere, so he likely moved in with her years ago. It's been about seven years since I last spoke to him, so he could easily be on the other side of the world."

"Do you have any way to find him?" Neil went into the kitchen and brought a package of

Oreos and a bag of sour cream and onion chips to the counter.

"I have one option." Gus popped a couple of chips into his mouth. "I have my grandma's old phone number. I can call her and see if she knows where to find him. I haven't spoken to her in several years, though, so it'll be awkward."

"Dude," Art said. "You're hunting down your father, whom you haven't seen in seven years. It's already awkward. Just do it!"

"Yea, give her a call," Mikey agreed. "We'll put a couple of pizzas in the oven for dinner, so call her and see what she knows."

Sighing, Gus stood up from the counter. He went outside, sat down on the front steps, and dialed the number saved under 'Grandma.' It rang a few times before an elderly woman answered.

"Hello?" she said.

"Hi, um, is this Lex Millburn?" he asked.

"Yes, this is her," the voice answered. "May I ask who is calling?"

"Grandma...it's Gus." An awkward silence followed his statement.

"Gus? I don't remember any Gus."

"I-I'm Brock's son."

"Brock's boy," she repeated slowly. "oh yes, I remember now! I'm terribly sorry. My memory isn't what it used to be, and it's been so long since you called."

"Yea, Grandma, I know. It's been a while.," he replied slowly. "I'm, um, sorry for not calling. Or visiting. I've, uh, been busy."

"I understand, sweetie. I'm just glad you called now," she agreed. "How are you doing?"

"I'm doing well. Um, I graduated from college last month, actually. A lot has happened since we last spoke."

"You graduated college? I didn't realize you had grown up so much. Congratulations! I wish you'd come by more often. I miss seeing you. Nobody visits much anymore." His grandma sighed forlornly on the other end of the line.

"I know, it's just…I've been busy," he said.

"Have you talked to your dad lately?" she asked. "How is he doing?"

"No, I haven't," Gus replied. "I haven't seen him since…since he married Joy. I don't even think I saw him after the engagement. We, uh, we stopped talking."

"That's unfortunate," his grandma said. "He and Joy were here for Easter. They brought her daughter with them. She was so pretty. I don't remember her name, though. They also had another kid with them, a boy who was about six years old. Your father played with him in the yard for hours. He really loves that boy."

Gus gritted his teeth and exhaled slowly. "They had a kid?"

"Yes, I think so. If I remember correctly, he introduced the boy as their son."

"Grandma, um, do you know where Brock lives? Or, or where he works? I wanted to talk to him, but I have no way to contact him."

Lex paused for a moment. "He works at Home Depot in Crawfordsville still. He's been there for several years. I don't know where he lives, but he should be up in the front office at Home Depot. He's been a manager there for a while now, so he supervises the night shift."

"Thanks Grandma. I'll look for him at Home Depot. I need to go now. Some friends are waiting for me."

"Okay, thanks for calling, Gus," she replied. "You should call more often."

"I'll...try. Bye Grandma." He hung up the phone and sat on the front steps for a while before going back inside.

"How'd it go?" Neil asked. "Judging from the look on your face, it wasn't pleasant."

"Yea, she did. We talked a little bit about life, but then Brock came up. Apparently he and Joy have a daughter. And a son. And according to Grandma, he really loves the kid." Gus took his seat, crossed his arms on the counter, and rested his head on his arms.

"Ouch, that sucks," Mikey noted. "How are you feeling?"

"Somewhere between completely heartbroken and absolutely pissed," Gus grumbled, his voice muffled. "He loves this little punk with some random woman, but not his first son? I did everything I could to make him a part of my life, and what does he do? He tosses me out and then kicks me while I'm down."

The room fell silent for a few minutes. Gus heard fidgeting in the kitchen but refused to lift his head. He sat unmoving, reflecting on all that had happened between Brock and him. All the conversations and encounters replayed in his head. He was lost in thought when Mikey set a plate of pizza in front of him.

"Eat, dude," he ordered. "Pizza makes everything better. And here's a Dew." He popped open a can and handed it to Gus, who lifted his head and accepted the food.

"I did learn something else," he remembered, stuffing a whole piece of pizza into his mouth. His friends waited as he chewed, swallowed, and washed it down with a swig of soda. "I learned that Brock works night at Home Depot in Crawfordsville. He's the night supervisor."

"Sweet!" Neil replied. "That's only like forty-five minutes from here. When do you want to go? Tonight or tomorrow?"

Gus considered his options as he ate another slice of pizza. "Let's go tonight. I want to get this over with. We can leave around midnight."

"Sounds like a plan," Mikey agreed.

The group continued eating in silence. Gus stared absentmindedly at the wall, thinking about the upcoming conversation.

"Have you written your letter yet?" Neil asked after a moment.

"No I haven't," Gus answered dryly. "I'm still figuring out what to say."

"Well what do you think what's-his-face from the Bad Dad Club would say if he were you?" Art asked. "From what you told us, his story seemed similar to yours."

"Well his name was Brandon," Gus replied. "And his response would be something about Jesus forgiving him or whatever."

"There was something else," Neil added. "He mentioned how he stopped hating his father and wanting to hurt him. Instead, he wanted him to be happy."

"Hmm," Gus grunted.

"Well I guess you have to ask yourself one question," Mikey said. "Are you in a place where you can honestly wish that for Brock?"

34

They moved to the garage and started a game of ping-ping with We Came As Romans blaring in surround sound. They played 'full court,' running around the garage and swinging wildly at the tiny plastic ball. Every few points, they stopped to take a drink and catch their breath. When midnight finally came, the group loaded their suitcases into the SUV and hit the road.

The drive was eerily silent. Neil played music through the radio, but nobody did more than lip-sync to it. Gus stared absently out the window at the passing scenery. None of his friends tried to start conversation, as they knew what he was feeling and thinking.

Within an hour, Mikey pulled into the parking lot at Home Depot. He parked at the back of the lot and turned off the ignition. They sat in silence for a moment.

Mikey sighed and turned to Gus. "How are you feeling? You ready?"

"I've wanted to vomit since I called my grandma. If the knots in my stomach get any tighter, I'll have a six-pack. I would much rather be anywhere else," he muttered. "But you guys already did it, so it's my turn." Without another word, he opened the door and stepped out. He led his friends into the empty store.

"What's he look like?" Neil asked. "We can split up and look for him. Or we can stay as a group and just have more eyes searching."

"Give me a sec," Gus replied. He opened Facebook on his phone and found Brock's profile. He was a middle-aged man with short, ashen hair, matching facial hair, and darkly tanned skin. "This is him." He showed his profile picture to the group, and they started wandering through the store.

After circling the store, they passed by the checkout lanes again. They had seen a couple of workers, but no Brock. Suddenly, Mikey tapped Gus on the shoulder and pointed at a man and woman talking by a register. Gus looked and recognized Brock.

"Well, here goes nothing," he grumbled, stepping into their lane. His father laughed heartily as he turned and saw Gus. His smile faded immediately, freezing Gus in place. Without a word, Brock shook his head and turned to walk away.

"Don't walk away from me!" Gus yelled, following him. "The least you could do is stop and listen to what I have to say!"

Brock stopped and faced Gus. "Why? I didn't ask you to come. I don't owe you anything."

"Then...walk away," Gus replied angrily. "You know how to do that. You, you have a wife and a daughter after all. Oh, and a son, if Grandma is correct."

"She shouldn't have told you that," Brock said. "That's none of your business." He turned around and started to walk away again.

"What's his name?" Gus shouted after him.

Brock paused and glanced over his shoulder. "Brandon. His name is Brandon."

"One last question." Gus hesitated and inhaled deeply. "Are, are you happy? With Joy, with your daughter, with Brandon? Is this the life you want?"

"Yes," Brock replied gruffly as he continued to walk.

Gus stood motionless for a moment, staring at the floor. He started to walk away but turned to look at Brock after a few steps.

"You better treat him better than me!" he shouted. "Treat Joy better than you treated Mom! Be the best husband and father you can be! And don't you ever, ever walk away from them! Make sure they know that they're loved! Be the father that you wanted as a kid!"

Gus watched as Brock continued walking, not even pausing to listen. He sighed and turned to his friends. Shrugging, they left Home Depot.

"Back to my house then?" Gus suggested. "I'm tired."

"Sounds good." Mikey pulled out of the parking lot as Gus returned to staring out the window.

35

Gus woke up the next morning and looked around his room groggily. Sunlight poured in through his windows, but his friends were nowhere to be seen. Grabbing his glasses, he staggered into the living room, where he found them watching *My Hero Academia*.

"What time is it?" he asked.

"Umm, like noon?" Neil guessed. "Something like that."

"You guys let me sleep this late?" Gus threw a pillow at Neil, suddenly alert.

"Hey!" Neil caught it and hurled it back. "We wanted to let you sleep off meeting Brock. Besides, it's summer! Relax and live a little!"

"Speaking of Brock, how are you feeling?" Mikey interrupted as Gus sat on the couch.

"I'm fine," he replied after a brief pause. "I'm actually surprised. When I saw Brock, I...I wasn't angry at all. I didn't want to shout at him or punch him. I just wanted to talk to him."

"That's good," Art said. "In fact, it's better than good. That's awesome. Definitely something to be proud of."

"Agreed!" Neil exclaimed. "You had an interesting conversation with Brock too. What made you ask him about his son and stuff?"

"Well you saw what happened when we found him," Gus explained. "He was talking to the cashier. He was laughing and having a good time until he saw me. Then he got all serious. That's when it dawned on me. It was selfish and immature to be vindictive, to want him to be miserable without me in his life. Seeing him happy made me realize that I was the one making myself miserable these last seven years, not him. He had moved on to a life that he loved."

"So you wanted to know about that life," Mikey said.

Gus nodded. "That's why I asked for his son's name. Then I remembered what we talked about yesterday, about Brandon wanting his father to be happy. I wanted to verify that he loves the life that he has."

"That makes sense," Art remarked. "If he abandoned you for a life that sucked, it would make your situation feel even worse."

"In a way," Neil added. "Now Gus knows that his father never actually loved him, that Brock ditched him for some random woman and a new family. I'm sure that sucks. What are you going to do now?"

"Have you seen *Dead Poets Society*?" Gus asked. "There's an early scene when Robin Williams's character is explaining the Latin phrase 'carpe diem.' 'Seize the day, boys,' he says. 'Make your lives extraordinary.' That's what I'm going to do. If Brock can live a full life without me, I can do the same without him."

"High five, man!" Neil exclaimed, leaning over Mikey and Art. "I realized the exact same thing, though I couldn't put it that nicely. Go us!"

"Do either of you know what that looks like for you?" asked. Neil and Gus exchanged looks and shrugged.

"Eh, we'll figure it out," Neil replied. The guys chuckled briefly before falling silent.

"I think...our road trip is done," Gus muttered. "I don't know about you guys, but I'm not really in the mood for more traveling and motels and junk food."

"I was thinking the same thing, to be honest," Mikey agreed.

"I mean, what could possibly top the insane week we just had?" Neil joked. "But yea, it was fun while it lasted. I think it's time to call it quits."

"What are we going to do now?" Art looked at each of his friends in turn. "Where do we go from here?"

"Well for me, I'm going to Tennessee," Mikey answered. "I know I've talked a lot about it, but Amber and I have some job and housing options lined up. So we're moving to Tennessee."

"That's awesome dude!" Neil exclaimed. "I think I'll work on my music. I can get back into a rhythm of practicing. I might even start posting stuff on YouTube to develop my own style and fan-base. I have a channel, but I haven't posted anything in a couple years. I can try to connect with other musicians there and get support and advice. That will help me have contacts once I graduate, so people will know how good I am."

"That's legit," Gus said. "I want to head west. Or east. Or anywhere, really. Get myself away from this town and everything that's happened here. I want something different. So I'm thinking of packing up the car, hitting the road, and seeing where that takes me. Then I'll settle down, get a job, and start a family. What about you, Art?"

"I'm going to go home and play video games," he said. "In all seriousness, I'll review my psych work so far. I want to make sure I know the material really well so that I can be the best counselor possible. Plus I should apply for my Master's in Counseling soon. But I hope to become more studious, kind of like what Dad wants. But it's not because Dad wants it. It's because I owe it to my future patients to be the best that I can be."

"Sounds like we all have lofty goals!" Mikey noted. "Too bad it means we're all going our separate ways. I'll be in Tennessee, Gus could end up anywhere, and who knows where you two will go when you graduate!"

"True, but none of that really matters," Gus argued. "We have Facebook and texting and other various social media. We can stay in touch without a problem. We can plan to visit one another for holidays or just for the fun of it."

"And we have this summer!" Art added. "We've made too many memories this summer to forget them! We'll have to go on a road trip again sometime."

"Or we could do something different," Mikey suggested. "A barbecue at my place. A trip to Universal. A cruise."

"Ooo, or a week in the mountains!" Gus said.

"I'm down, but on one condition," Neil replied. "We can't visit our dads or anything emotional like that again. None of that."

"Deal!" his friends agreed, laughing.

36

Mikey, Art, and Neil stayed for another night. They spent the day brainstorming ideas for future trips. Ruby returned home and prepared a full dinner of ham, macaroni and cheese, and green beans. After dinner, they retreated to Gus's room to watch anime.

The next morning, Mikey decided it was time to leave. They cleaned out the SUV and then packed and loaded their suitcases. They then found themselves standing in the driveway, prolonging the goodbyes.

"I've been thinking," Neil said after a moment of silence.

"About what?" Gus asked, kicking the gravel absentmindedly.

"Something Matt said. He mentioned that the statistics for a fatherless kid aren't good. Most of them end up in jail, addicted to drugs or alcohol, as early parents, or worse. Admittedly the odds were slightly better for Art and Mikey, but they weren't favorable for any of us."

"What's your point?" Mikey asked.

"We beat those odds," Neil replied. "We should be in prison or on drugs or dead or whatever, because your dads sucked. But we didn't. Against all odds, we turned out alright. Despite all the hell that they put us through, we're okay. Not only did we survive, but we *thrived*. Yes, we still have our bad days like anybody else. But overall, even on our worst days, we're okay."

"Hmm, that's a good point," Art agreed. "Maybe we aren't always doing well, but at our worst, we're still better than we could've been. We're still okay."

"That reminds me," Mikey said. "I've been thinking about something my dad said. He made that comment about not raising me as well as my grandpa raised him. Almost like he tried to raise me the exact same way."

"That's interesting," Neil replied. "Maybe he didn't realize that there was a better way to be a dad, so he went with what he knew."

"Yea, that makes sense," Mikey said. "I'll just have to find the better way, now that I know it's out there."

"*We'll* have to find the better way," Art added.

"Touché," Gus agreed. "I've also been thinking about what Brandon said. About his story and being able to forgive his dad."

"What about it?" Mikey asked.

"I should get back to church stuff. I was so into the Bible and stuff in middle school, but I let myself fall away when Brock left. I want that back in my life."

"That's pretty noble," Art said. "There's plenty of good stuff in the Bible about being a good dad, too. I should read it more too. That's something we can do together!"

"Yes!" Mikey exclaimed. "Let's do it!"

The men looked at Neil, who shrugged. "Sure, I'm in. We'll discuss where to start and stuff sometime soon."

"How about you three figure that out on the way home?" Mikey suggested. "I hate to cut this party short, but we gotta go. It'll be like 7 or 8 hours until I get home."

The three men exchanged hugs and goodbyes with Gus before climbing into Mikey's SUV one last time. When the vehicle disappeared from his line of sight, Gus returned to his bedroom and sat at his desk. He spun in his chair for a moment before noticing an envelope on his bedside table.

Sighing, Gus opened the envelope and pulled out the blank sheet of paper inside. He grabbed a pen and sat in silence for a moment before writing six words.

"Dear Brock, I'm glad you're happy."

He returned the paper to the envelope and tucked it into his center desk drawer. He reclined in his chair for a moment, staring at the drawer, before he started spinning again.

Epilogue

The doorbell rang. Amber left the kitchen and opened to door to find Gus and Charlie with their daughters.

"Oh my goodness, hi!" Amber exclaimed, hugging Gus and Charlie quickly. She knelt to talk to the girls. "Hello Jerica and Micah! You two have gotten so big!"

"Hi Aunt Amber," Jerica said, hugging her. "I'm five now." She proudly held up five fingers.

"You are? That's so exciting! Did you have a good birthday?"

"Yea, Mommy and Daddy took me on a picnic at the park."

"That's so cool! Micah, can I have a hug?"

"No," she said, hiding behind Gus's leg.

"You know Aunt Amber," Charlie said. "Don't you want to give her a hug?" Micah shook her head no and tugged on Gus's pant leg.

"She'll be okay in a bit," Gus said, picking her up. "Art and Aly should be right behind us. They probably stopped for a soda or something. I assume Mikey's in the back?"

"You are correct!" Amber replied, leading the group inside. "He's almost done with the meat. I'm just finishing up the beans and slaw. Lunch should be ready in about 5."

"Sweet. I'm going to make sure he doesn't burn the place down. Micah, do you want to stay in here with Mommy and Aunt Amber?" His daughter shook her head no and buried her face in his shoulder.

"I'll be right behind you, love," Charlie said. "I'm going to help Amber finish up here."

"I'm gonna go outside with Daddy," Jerica interrupted, walking after him.

"Is that how you talk to Mommy? Do you tell Mommy what you're going to do?" Charlie knelt to look her daughter in the eyes.

"No," she replied slowly. "May I go outside with Daddy?"

"Of course, sweetheart. Go have fun with your cousins." Charlie patted Jerica on the head gently and grinned.

Gus stepped onto the back patio. In the yard, Ezra played tag with his younger sisters. Mikey stood at the grill and watched them play contently. Jerica exited the house and quickly joined the game.

"Gus, my man!" Mikey exclaimed, hurrying to hug him. "And sweet little Micah! How are you, sweetie?" Micah grunted in objection and looked away from him.

"She's being shy today," Gus explained. "Typical toddlers. She'll be fine before long."

"Oh yea, I remember when Abby and Emmie were like that. It drove their brother crazy!" Gus and Mikey chuckled.

"I believe it. What's for lunch?"

"You know what they say: when in Rome!" Mikey raised the lid of the grill.

"Ah, brisket!" Gus noted. "Delicious! How long has it been smoking?"

"About twelve hours. It's gonna be so juicy and delicious! I can't wait."

The back door opened, and two young boys ran out. They crossed the yard and started talking to Ezra, who stopped playing with the girls. The girls seemed not to notice, as they kept running and tagging each other. Art and Alyson stepped outside after them.

"Hey guys!" Aly greeted. "Good to see you all!" The four of them exchanged hugs.

"Micah!" Art exclaimed. "Come see your Uncle Art!" He held his hands out to her. She looked at him for a second before turning away.

"Hey, that's more than she's done for anybody else today! How was the drive?" Gus shifted Micah to his other arm.

"Long. Why is Texas so huge?" Art replied. "It felt like we drove forever!"

"It just is, man," Mikey answered. "Deal with it. I didn't draw the state lines."

"Dad!" Ezra shouted, running over to the group. "Can I get the football to throw around with Danny and Gabe?"

"Sure," Mikey said. "We may even join you in a second!"

"Awesome! Thanks!" The boy ran to the shed at the corner of the yard and came out with a football, which he tossed to one of Art's boys.

"When did he get so big?" Aly asked. "It seems like he was Micah's size just last year!"

"You're telling me!" Mikey said. "He's the tallest kid in third grade! He's also super mature. He's been inviting all his friends to come to church without us even suggesting it. He just realized that Jesus was too important to keep to himself."

"That's pretty rad," Art remarked. "Gabe and Danny are a little shy for that. But their teachers have told us that they stick up for the littler kids during recess. Let them join the big kid games, teach them how to play."

"Most of the time," Aly added.

Gus chuckled. "Of course. They are kids, after all. They can be super mature one second and ornery brats the next."

"Oh you have no idea," Mikey scoffed. "Your kids are still young. You'll see it more as they get older. But teaching them to be more mature and less ornery is all part of parenting."

Conversation paused as Emmie walked up to her brother and tugged on his shirt. They spoke briefly before he knelt and handed her the football. He helped her toss it to Abby, who ran up to join the new game excitedly. The older boys cheered when Emmie tossed the ball, then Danny retrieved it to help Abby return the pass.

"I want to play, I want to play!" Jerica shouted, chasing after the ball. Abby and Danny passed the ball, which bounced off her head. She stood stunned for a moment before turning to look at Gus, tears welling up.

"Now sweetie, what's Daddy's rule?" he asked her from the patio. "Are you okay?"

"Don't freak out," she shouted back. "Yea, I'm okay, Dad." Rubbing her forehead, she turned around and quickly returned to playing catch.

"Play," Micah said suddenly, pointing towards the other kids.

"You want to play? Do you want Daddy to hold you while you play?"

"Yes. Hold yous!"

"Okay." Gus glanced at his friends. "Feel free to join me."

Aly followed Gus onto the lawn as Mikey and Art chatted at the grill. Gus raised his hand to receive the ball.

"Here you go, Uncle Gus!" Danny said, tossing the ball gently.

"Thanks Danny! Are you ready to throw it, Micah?" She grabbed the ball excitedly. "Let go of the ball on three. One…two…three!" Gus pivoted his torso a couple times as he counted, and Micah pushed the ball away from her. Gabe ran forward and rolled into the grass to catch it. Micah laughed and clapped her hands.

"I'm glad our kids get along so well," Gus noted. "Especially as they've gotten older."

"For now," Aly replied. "They'll be at each other's throats in an hour if they don't get their space. But it definitely helps that they're so close in age and that they see each other so often."

"True. This annual cookout was a good idea. It gives us all an excuse to stop what we're doing and hang out."

"Well it would be easier if you all moved down here!" Mikey shouted.

"Or you and Amber could move back up north!" Aly retorted.

"Yea, what she said!" Art seconded.

"Abby, Emmie, it's time for lunch!" Amber shouted. "Come sit down while Mom and Dad get your plates!" The girls all ran to the patio table and claimed their seats while Mikey, Amber, and Charlie made their plates.

"Let's go boys!" Aly echoed, catching the football and setting it on the ground. Danny and Gabe followed Ezra to the patio and grabbed plates.

"Do you want me to make Micah's plate?" Charlie asked as Gus approached the patio.

"Mommy food!" Micah shouted excitedly, wriggling in Gus's arms.

"I'll take that as a yes," Charlie replied. "Do you want to eat with Mommy or Daddy?"

Micah looked back and forth at her parents. "Umm Daddy."

"Hey Art, do me a solid and make me a plate, bro!" Gus requested, taking a seat.

"You got it!" he said. Art delivered Gus's plate before sitting down with his own. Charlie sat down next to him and slid a plate in front of Micah, who quickly reached for a piece of brisket.

"Hold on sweetie," Charlie said gently, putting her hand on top of Micah's. "What do we do before we eat?"

"Pray!" she said excitedly. She put her hands in her lap and waited as Mikey, Amber, and Aly sat down.

"Who wants to say grace?" Mikey asked.

"I'll do it!" Gus volunteered. Everyone bowed their heads. "Father God, thank you for safe travel, good food, and even better family. Bless this food to nourish our bodies, and bless this time to glorify you. In Jesus's name, amen."

"Amen," everybody repeated. The children immediately started eating.

"Before the meal gets too crazy, we have something that we want to say!" Gus said loudly, looking around the table.

"Jerica, sweetie, do you remember what Mommy and Daddy told you?" Charlie asked.

"Uuum no?" she replied slowly, confused.

"What are you and sissy going to be next year?" Charlie asked.

"Uuum."

"You're going to be big somethings," Gus said, grinning broadly.

"Big sisters!" Jerica exclaimed. "We're going to be big sisters!"

Everyone at the table froze.

"Wait, you mean--?" Aly began.

"Yep!" Gus said, beaming. "We're having another baby!"

The table erupted with congratulations and excitement. Micah shouted and pounded the table with her fists energetically.

"That's so awesome!"

"Congratulations!"

"When are you due?"

"When did you find out?"

"Boy or girl?"

"How many more are you going to have?"

"Have you picked out names yet?"

"I hope it's a boy!"

"Well I hope it's another girl!"

"Easy now, everyone," Gus said, raising his hand. "She was late about six weeks ago, but we waited until we saw the doctor and knew with certainty. We called our parents first, obviously, then decided to wait until our get-together to tell you all."

"As for boy or girl," Charlie added, "we don't know. Jerica and Micah were both surprises, so we're doing the same for this one."

"I hope it's another girl," Gus admitted. "But we'll find out early next year."

"That's so awesome," Mikey repeated.

"We have to toast to this!" Art exclaimed.

"Let's do it!" Aly agreed, raising her drink.

"To Gus and Charlie's new baby!" everyone exclaimed, raising their drinks.

The table exploded with laughter and conversation as the meal resumed.

Special Thanks

First, I need to thank my initial readers. These folks have read my manuscript from the first draft to publication (and put up with my nagging every step of the way). There are several of you, so I'll thank you each in turn:

- To Squirt: Thanks for being insane and reading the first draft in 36 hours. Thanks for sharing my manuscript with close friends too, both with and without permission.

- Sloth: Thanks for making time in your life to read my novel. I know you were busy with working full-time, being married, and then having a kid. Congrats on that, and thanks for being such a supportive friend.

- To J: Thanks for being special; you received the manuscript before anyone else in our circle of friends. Thanks for loving John Green and being excited and encouraging about my pursuits as an author.

- To Casey: Thanks for inspiring me to take my writing seriously. Thanks for providing much constructive criticism about my work, including the best comment ever: "Y'know, this kind of rocks!"

Thanks to the folks at NaNoWriMo. If not for the challenge you provide every year, I don't know when I would have gotten to writing this story. Thanks for pushing me out of my comfort zone and motivating me to chase my dream.

Thanks to everyone who encouraged me along the way, on Facebook, Twitter, or Instagram. It means a lot that so many people in my life not only want me to pursue life as an author but to excel in that life. Even if I never formally met you, if you encouraged me along the way, thanks so much.

Lastly, this may seem cliché, but thank you to all readers. Whether friends, family, fans, or complete strangers, thanks for taking time to read a story that is so close to my heart. I love you and look forward to providing more stories that entertain and educate.

30264734R00192

Made in the USA
Columbia, SC
25 October 2018